Story Box

Story Box

Short Stories

Paul Curd

GUILTON PRESS

A CIP catalogue record for this book is available from the British Library.
ISBN 9780955961120

www.paulcurd.co.uk

For Denise

Contents

Gun

Next thing I know I'm standing in the shadows of a doorway. I'm wearing a trench coat and a fedora pulled down low, like Sam Spade or Philip Marlowe. It's five o'clock in the evening and it's already dark. I'm cold. There's a light drizzle in the evening air.

She comes out the office block just after five, just like she's supposed to, and makes for the tube. The streets are awash with citizens leaving work, a flood of humanity hurrying home. I breaststroke through them. Some creep jostles me and I think, *Don't you know who I am?* If I had more time I'd make sure a nasty surprise came his way, but lucky for him I have more pressing things on my mind just now.

She walks into the station and I follow her through the barrier and down the escalator onto the platform. There are so many characters pressing to get on the train that it's easy for me to tail her pretty close without her being any the wiser. Plus she's easy to spot, with her refulgent blonde hair and her elegant model's poise. She reminds me of Kim Basinger looking like Veronica Lake in L A Confidential. She's the most glamorous woman in the train carriage, that's for sure. She looks up unexpectedly and I swear she's smiling at me. You know, the sort of smile that makes you wish you were wearing roomier jeans. I look away.

We get to Belsize Park and she's on the move. It's tougher to follow her up on the surface because there's less populace about. But I know where she lives so I just hang back and try to look casual. She acts completely normal, does exactly what she's supposed to do. I can't understand it. If it's not her it must be Steve. It must be Steve.

I keep watching her until she's safe inside her apartment, then I hail a passing taxi and give directions to Steve's house, a smart place up Highgate way. He's a widower and he lives alone. I know it's unprofessional but I've grown quite fond of poor Steve, and I've even begun to feel guilty about having killed his wife. It was nothing personal. I was just doing my job. Of course, he doesn't know it was me that killed her. In fact, he doesn't even know me, doesn't even have an inkling that I exist. But I know him. And I like him anyway.

Cardinal rule: don't get involved, just do what you have to do and walk away. You need that infamous splinter of ice in your heart.

I still feel guilty, though. Which is probably why I wanted him to meet the blonde, partly to go some way towards making it up to him (yeah, I know it's a poor trade) but also, and more importantly, because it's all part of my grand plan. You see, I'm fed up with all this scrabbling around in the dark. I've been plotting the Big One, my break into the big time, and Steve's a key part of it.

But for some reason he isn't playing ball.

At Steve's place I tell the cab driver to wait and keep the fare ticking. I go up to the front door and let myself in with my skeleton key. It's dark in the hallway, which suits me fine. I slip into the shadows and sneak along to the kitchen. Steve is sitting at the table, staring blankly into space. There's a glass and a bottle of bourbon on the table, but no indication that anything is going on in his head. I look him over. He's a lot like me: a little taller, perhaps; a bit

2

younger. More good looking, certainly, with what I can only describe as 'rugged features'.

I watch him, but nothing happens. He's wearing the kind of expression on his rugged face that makes you think he'd be happy to put a bullet through his temple. That's not right. It's not part of my plan. He should have gotten over the death of his wife by now. He should be ready for the hot relationship I've lined up for him with the blonde. He should be getting ready for the date with her tonight. But he's not playing along.

I want to walk into the kitchen and grab hold of his shoulders, give him a good shaking up. But I can't. I have to use the blonde. I have to make her try harder.

So I leave Steve in his kitchen and take the cab back to her apartment. I pull up the collar of my trench coat and pull down the brim of my hat. This time, though, rather than lurk in the shadows I hang about right underneath the lamppost so she can easily spot me, standing in a soft pool of orange light. After a while she parts the curtains of her bedroom window and peeps out. I want her to know I'm watching her. I want her to get the message.

She gets the message all right. Half a minute later she comes downstairs and opens the door. She leans seductively against the frame, like the femme fatale she is.

'Are you going to stand there all night?' she says. Her voice is aural velvet. She's wearing a pink satin dressing gown that somehow accentuates all the things it hides. 'Or are you coming in?'

I don't have to think too hard. She leads me straight upstairs to her bedroom, deep red drapes and erotic prints. The bedside lamps give off a sultry glow, and the air is thick with the sweet scent of expectation. I notice there's a heavy black revolver on her dressing table, the kind of snub-nosed handgun popular in 70s cop movies. I wonder where the hell it came from, and a half-remembered quote comes into my head – was it Chekhov? – some rule about writers putting guns on tables. But then the blonde shrugs off her dressing gown and I'm distracted by her perfect air-brushed body. She begins to remove my clothes, each button popping unhindered from its buttonhole, my jeans simply falling from my hips, and I'm protesting weakly that this isn't right as I cup her firm breasts in my eager hands.

'What did you expect would happen when you came here?' she murmurs, breathless. 'This is what you really want, isn't it?'

We're in her bed now, all silk and satin, and she's open and receptive and I know it's unforgivable but I just can't help myself.

'Isn't that what you were after all along?' she whispers afterwards, her lips soft against my ear. 'I know you wanted me to fall for Steve, but how could I? He's so one-dimensional! The man has no depth, no personality. I can't even be sure what he looks like! My God, "rugged features"? What the hell does that mean? Surely you could have done better than that! You should have spent more time on developing his character and less time thinking about me. After all, I'm just the love interest. I don't even have a name!'

Suddenly her bedroom door crashes open, and there's Steve, glowering on the threshold, his rugged features darkened by some kind of Freudian anger. I know he knows who I am, and that I killed his wife. He knows I was the one who gave her the tumour and then fixed her up with an incompetent surgeon. And I know now why there's a gun on the dressing table, cocked and loaded.

And I know what has to happen next.

4

The Ten Shilling Note

The ten shilling note fluttered down like a large brown moth, then swooped under the table where the boy was sitting cross-legged. It fluttered again one last time, and finally came to rest on the linoleum floor beside his knee. The boy held his breath. He looked at the ten shilling note, then at his mother's unmoving American Tan legs. She was standing at the kitchen table, counting out the money she had saved in the tin from the dresser. The boy was pretending it was the Blitz and the bombs were raining down. When their house was hit the ceiling would collapse, but he would be the only one to survive, safe under the heavy kitchen table. Ka-boom!

But, instead of wood and plaster falling all around him, it was a ten shilling note. He waited for his mother to bend down to retrieve it. Her feet, though, in their slippers with the pink fluffy edging, did not move. He could hear her counting under her breath: 'Eighteen, nineteen, nineteen and six, nineteen and ninepence, seven pounds.'

The boy picked up the ten shilling note. A thrill charged him as he held it between his fingers, feeling the peculiar texture of the paper, examining the picture of Britannia.

'Seven pounds three and fourpence,' said his mother out loud, as if she intended him to hear, as if she were prompting him to speak up. 'I'd've thought there should've been a bit more than that. There's not much more than last week.'

The boy looked at the ten shilling note one last time. He drew in a breath to say something.

'Oh well,' his mother said. 'Can't be helped.'

He heard her scooping up the coins and dropping them into the empty tin. He heard the rustle of paper money being pushed in, the metallic pop of the lid being closed. His mother's slippers turned and her legs moved, one in front of the other, to the dresser. He watched her stretch up onto tiptoes, heard the clump and scrape of the tin on the top shelf.

The boy was panting with excitement. His mother had no idea she had dropped the ten shilling note. *Finders keepers*, he thought. He read the inscription: *I promise to pay the bearer on demand.* 'The bearer'. That was him now. His chest began to pound.

'Philip!' his mother called out suddenly, startling him so that his head crashed against the underside of the table. 'Philip! Where are you?'

Little stars swam and exploded before his eyes. 'I'm down here,' he called back, rubbing his crown. The ten shilling note fell from his hand.

'What on earth are you doing under there?'

There was laughter in her voice as she bent her knees to look below the table. Without thinking, Philip snatched up the banknote and stuffed it into the pocket of his shorts.

'Will you run an errand for me, Philip, dear?'

He got to his feet, but his gaze remained fixed on her slippers.

'Brenda will be here in a minute and I've run out of ciggies. Pop round to Kendrick's for me, will you? I'll give you a penny for going.'

She held out half a crown. It was shining brightly in the light from the window, freshly minted with the new Queen's head on it. The words formed in his head, *It's all right, Mum. I've got the ten bob you dropped.* But the words never quite made the journey from his brain to his

6

mouth. He took the big silver coin and turned away, sick with guilt. He could feel the all-seeing eyes of his Father-Who-Art-In-Heaven burning down into his soul. He hurried to the door.

'Wait a minute, Philip!'

She knew! She had been waiting for him to tell her the truth and he never had. Now she would slap his legs for telling lies and send him to bed without any supper. Tears stung his eyes. He heard her pull open the dresser drawer and push it shut again.

'You'd better get me a box of matches an' all.'

Philip ran to Kendrick's as fast as his thin white legs would carry him. He knew he had had a lucky escape. He had got away with the theft so far, but the fear of discovery was almost too much to bear. He imagined a policeman making him turn out his pockets and finding the note. How would a seven year old come by a ten bob note unless through theft? Philip had to get rid of the evidence. As he ran he formulated a desperate plan. If he paid for his mum's cigarettes with the ten shilling note he could keep the half-crown his mum had given him, plus seven and six from the change from the banknote, and then he would still have ten bob but the evidence of the banknote would be gone. He would be in the clear.

At the top of his street, just where it joined the main road, was an old horse-trough that was still used occasionally by the rag and bone man's nag. Philip spat in it for luck as he ran past. He was sure his plan would work. He took the corner at full tilt, and made it to Kendrick's in record time.

'Whoa! Where's the fire?' The man behind the counter was new, a small and wiry man with a face that made Philip think of *The Wind in the Willows*. Ratty. He had black hair greased back with lots of Brylcreem. There was a thin moustache above his upper lip that looked to Philip as if it had been drawn on with an eyeliner pencil. Philip peered beyond him through the doorway into the room at the back. Old Mr Kendrick was sitting at a table, smoking his pipe and reading this week's *Reveille*. He looked up when the Rat Man said, 'Well, well, well. It's young Philip, ain't it? You ain't changed much.'

Philip wished Old Mr Kendrick would come through to serve him, but instead he called out, 'You all right there, Stanley?'

The Rat Man said, 'Yes, Dad.' He grinned at Philip with teeth that went brown at the ends. 'Don't suppose you remember me, do you? I been away.'

Philip shook his head, but there was something familiar about the Rat Man's features.

'How's your mum, Philip? She ain't been down the *Palais* lately. Stopped going has she, since I went away?'

Philip looked hard at his moustache, trying to see if it was made of bristles or pencil. 'Where did you go away to? Did you go on holiday?'

The Rat Man roared at that. 'On holiday? Yeah, that's right, son. I been to a special holiday camp on the Isle of Wight.'

'We're saving up to go to Butlins!' said Philip. His pride and excitement were deadened by the guilt of the ten shilling note. It was evidence that could be held against him. He took out the banknote and thrust it in the Rat Man's direction. 'Twenty Kensitas, please,' he said. 'And a box of matches.'

'Tell your mum I'm back,' the Rat Man said as he turned to take the cigarettes from the rack behind him. 'Tell her Stan the Man's back in town.'

He handed the cigarettes to the boy. 'Keep your money, son. Tell your mum Stan said she could have them for nothing. My treat.'

'No!' said Philip, so loud that old Mr Kendrick looked up from his paper. 'No, she wanted change. She told me to ask for coins for the meter.'

'Did she now?' said Stanley, handing over the box of matches, still not relieving Philip of the stolen banknote. 'Tell her I ain't got no change at the moment. Tell her I'll have some later if she wants to pop in herself. Will you tell her that?'

Philip took the cigarettes and matches and left the shop with an immense feeling of disappointment at his failure. When he got back to the horse-trough there was a figure propped against the water pump, a man wearing RAF uniform under a flying jacket. He was tall and handsome, with a heroic scar across his brow. He was still wearing his pilot's helmet. Philip knew it was his father without having to be introduced. Squadron Leader James Bigglesworth, DSO, DFC and bar, of 266 Squadron. His Father-Who-Art-in-Heaven, come down to Earth again. He was smoking a cigarette and whistling *We'll Meet Again*. Philip slowed to a stop, half-deaf from the pounding of his heart in his ears.

'Chin up, old son,' his father said. 'It can't be as bad as all that.'

With some difficulty, Philip's father shifted his weight from the pump and hauled himself upright. He smiled in a way that made everything suddenly seem all right. But there was a dreadful dark hole under the arm of the flying jacket from which there trickled a trail of purple-coloured blood.

'Does it hurt?' Philip said.

'Not any more, old son. Not any more.'

9

He took one last drag on his cigarette before flicking the butt into the trough. Philip heard the hiss. He breathed in the dark scent of tobacco and whiskey and aircraft engine oil and cordite and shrapnel and blood.

'So what's the score with the ten bob? You know it doesn't belong to you.'

Philip hung his head in shame.

'I'm disappointed in you, old son. Have you ever known me to steal? It's dashed dishonourable. And stand to attention when I'm speaking to you!'

'Yes, sir.' Philip puffed out his chest, arms stiff at his sides.

'You'd best come clean, Philip. You'd best hand the money back to your mother like a good boy. Don't you think?'

'Yes, sir.'

'Okay. Well, close your eyes and make a wish . . .'

Philip closed his eyes and wished his dad hadn't been killed in the war, and when he opened his eyes Squadron Leader Biggles was gone.

His mum's friend, Brenda, was sitting at the kitchen table, drinking tea and smoking, when Philip got back. His mother was sitting opposite Brenda and with her back to the door. She was saying something about knitting and hot baths, and wishing she could have afforded the gin, but Brenda cut across her with a loud, 'Hello-o, Phil!'

'Speak of the Devil,' his mum said. 'Did you get my ciggies?'

'I saw my dad!' Philip blurted.

His mum, who had half-turned in her chair, seemed to choke.

Brenda said, 'Yeah, I heard he was out. Bad news–'

'Brenda!' Philip's mum said, whipping back to face her. 'He can't've seen his dad. His dad was killed in the war. Remember?'

'The war?' said Brenda. 'The last war?'

'Yes,' said Philip, stepping forward to defend his dad in case Brenda suggested he was anything less than the greatest war hero the country had ever seen. 'He was shot down. He was killed flying Spitfires in the Battle of Britain.'

'The Battle of Britain? The Battle of Britain in 1940?' She began to laugh so much she had a coughing fit, blue smoke blowing everywhere.

His mother got out of her chair and came to squat down beside him. 'You couldn't've seen him then, could you Philip, dear? Not if he was killed in the war?'

'He came down from Heaven to speak to me! He's been watching over me!'

His mum gave him a sad smile. 'You mustn't tell stories, Philip. It's naughty to tell lies, and we know what happens to naughty boys, don't we?'

'But it's true!' He slammed the cigarettes and matches onto the table and dug his hand deep into the pocket of his shorts. 'I can prove it!'

He began to chant the Lord's Prayer to himself, and pulled out the ten shilling note. His mum gasped and gripped hold of the chair back.

'He told me to give you this,' Philip said.

'W – what for?'

'It's for the holiday. It's for Butlin's.'

His mum sat down on her chair in slow motion. She couldn't speak. Then, without warning, she began to cry. Not quietly, but loud as a baby. Brenda came round the table to comfort her, giving Philip a stern look as if he had been to blame for whatever it was his mum was crying about.

'If he thinks . . .' his mum snivelled, when the wailing had died down. 'If he thinks I would ever . . . he can't just . . . I thought I'd seen the last . . .'

Without knowing why, Philip began to cry, too. He didn't know what was wrong with his mum, but he could tell Brenda was right. It was all his fault. He took a step forward to lay his hand on his mum's shoulder, but she turned suddenly towards him.

'Leave me alone!' she shouted. 'Leave me alone, and go to your bed and stay there. I can't bear to look at you!'

Philip ran up the passage, wild and blinded by stinging tears and the terrible pain inside him. He didn't know why his mum had been so angry with him. He didn't understand why she didn't want to see his father again. He didn't understand anything. His father had been wrong to tell him to return the ten shilling note. He should have kept it, and none of this would have happened. And then he remembered the half-crown he still had in his pocket. And he knew, as he threw himself on his little bed in the corner of his mum's bedroom, that he would not tell his mum about it. He would keep it secret. He would keep the money for himself.

And he would never, ever give his mum the message from the Rat Man.

The Stain

First thing on Monday morning she had a bath and caught the bus into town. It took a lot of nerve, but she did it. The whole way there her heart was thudding; she was afraid one of the other passengers might recognise her. She'd had a fright when she first got on the bus, and the driver had given her a long look. But he was only flirting.

'Haven't seen you on my bus before,' he said, giving her a wink as he took her money.

'No,' she said, taking her ticket and hurrying to find a seat.

It was good to sit down. She had been on her feet since Friday, packing away and getting things ready in London, then unpacking again and sorting things out down here. It had taken her the whole weekend to get the house straight enough to feel comfortable in, and that was just the kitchen, the living room and her bedroom. Someone had told her it would take a year before she got the last box unpacked. The dining room was still a mess, full of crates of crockery and ornaments and pictures, and the spare bedroom had become the storage area for everything else.

Her new neighbours seemed friendly enough, but she'd been warned to stay on her toes. Country folk liked to know more about you than people who lived in London. You couldn't call it nosiness; it was all part of living out in the country, the community spirit. It was what village life was all about. Nevertheless, she knew she had to be careful.

The house she bought was anonymous and unobtrusive, a plain cottage on the outskirts of the village. It was the start of her new life, she told herself as she unpacked her suitcases and put her clothes away in her new bedroom. No more looking over her shoulder. No more living in fear. She felt safe knowing that nobody here knew her. She could start again. As she unpacked she tossed aside the things that could do with a clean. There was still blood on her jacket . . .

'Ann Singleton,' Ann had said, introducing herself to the old lady from next door when she called soon after the removal men had gone, offering tea and biscuits. 'But just call me Ann.'

'You're on your own then,' the old lady said.

'I'm a widow,' Ann had said, truthfully. 'I've only recently . . . I thought I'd make a clean break.'

'From London, are you?'

'Neasden,' Ann said, and immediately regretted it. She was already giving too much away. Even though she was just an old lady, Ann knew she had to be more careful. If people found out . . .

'Oh,' the old lady said, not making the connection. 'Nice.'

She had to be more careful. 'Ann Singleton,' she said to herself as she stepped from the bus. 'My name is Ann Singleton.'

The town was a faded seaside resort looking out over the cold grey English Channel. And as she walked along the main street, her clothes bundled under her arm in an old carrier bag, the sun came out. The scene was transformed. The Channel came to life, sparkling and twinkling in the sudden light. The shops were no longer dowdy but bright and welcoming. This is a sign, she thought. From now on, everything in my life will be sunny.

The dry cleaner's shop was hot and stuffy, the air dense and chemical-sweet. Rows of plastic-wrapped clothes hung on rails on either side. Behind the counter was a price list

14

on a partition wall that cut off the shop area from the fume-filled cleaning area at the back. She could hear voices from in there, a man and a woman, arguing. Ann pinged the dome-shaped bell on the counter and waited. The arguing stopped and a middle-aged woman pushed through the plastic bead curtain and smiled.

The woman gave her a timid smile, a kindred spirit. Ann knew what it was like to be bullied and harassed. The woman took the dresses and skirts, the salmon-pink jacket with the dark stain on the breast, and attached little blue tickets to them.

'Do you need them in a hurry?' She spoke with a soap opera voice, part Walford, part Ramsey Street.

Ann said she didn't.

The man called from the back, sharply demanding the woman's presence.

'Excuse me,' she said with her timid smile, and passed back through the bead curtain. Ann could hear the man barking something, the woman quietly responding. Ann's jacket was lying abandoned on the counter. She could see the dark brown stain, and it made her shiver. She folded the jacket so the stain was hidden.

'It'll probably be the end of the week?' the woman said, returning. She said it as if were a question, and Ann wondered whether that was just the way she spoke or if she was really asking whether a week would be all right. She said the end of the week was fine.

A tousle-haired man with hairy shoulders in a white vest stepped from the fume-filled rear of the shop carrying an armful of bagged-up garments.

'So they'll be ready on Friday?' the woman said, taking down Ann's details on the counterfoil of her receipt book. Ann was distracted, watching the man as he placed the clothing on the rails. He was big, hugely obese, with a

15

scowling face. He looked as if he'd been pumped up with air, over inflated, and that he was angry about it. His vest was damp with sweat, his hair plastered to his wet scalp.

'Sorry?' Ann said.

'Friday morning.' She handed Ann the receipt.

There was something about the dry cleaner that reminded her of Harry. Not physically – Harry had been a slim man – but in his bullying demeanour, the way he treated his shop assistant. She didn't like the way he had made her think of Harry.

She needed some air.

Ann walked along the beach for a while, crunching through the shingle and watching the waves break noisily on the pebbles before hissing away again. She even walked to the end of the ugly concrete pier, watching the men fishing, waving at a passing crabber.

Harry had always been violent. It was in his nature, it ran in his family. His brothers were as bad. The three of them had always had a reputation for being hard men. But they were getting older, and Harry had started bringing his frustrations home, taking them out on Ann. When she killed him it had been in self-defence, clean and simple. The judge had even sympathised with her. Harry's brothers didn't see it that way. There was family honour at stake. If they ever tracked her down . . .

On the way back to the bus stop she passed a hairdresser and, on a whim, went inside to book an appointment for a new style. A completely new look.

'And the name?' said the blonde girl on reception duties.

The name. Ann nearly said Johnson, an automatic response. But she remembered just in time. 'Um, it's Singleton,' she said, spelling it out as much for her own sake as for the blonde girl. Ann watched her write out the unfamiliar name. She could see now that the girl was a bottle blonde, her dark roots showing as she hunched over the appointments book.

'I wonder how I would look blonde?' Ann thought, as she sat on the top deck home.

That afternoon the phone in the hall began to ring, making her jump. It was her first phone call in her new home. She wondered who could be calling her. She was half afraid to answer it. Eventually, she picked up the receiver, said her new number into the mouthpiece.

'Hello?' said a stern male voice. 'Is that Mrs Johnson?'

'W-What?'

'Is that Mrs Johnson? Mrs Ann Johnson?'

'No!' said Ann, slamming the phone down before the man could say any more. Her heart was pounding, cold sweat pricking her. Someone had tracked her down! She'd been here for less than two days, barely forty eight hours, and already someone had tracked her down! The phone began to ring again, but Ann couldn't move. It rang and rang. Tears were burning her eyes. Would it never stop?

Eventually it did.

It had all been for nothing. Selling up and moving away from her friends, her familiar surroundings. All for nothing. She felt she would go mad!

She left the phone off the hook for the rest of the day, the hall door closed against the infuriating beeping alert. 'I *know* it's off the hook!' she shouted at it more than once, her nerves frayed. Eventually, even the bleeping stopped.

She slept badly. But the next morning she resolved to face up to it. She replaced the handset on the cradle. Nothing happened. She allowed herself a long, luxurious sigh of relief. She had expected it to ring instantly, but it didn't make a sound.

Not until just after ten o'clock, anyway.

'Mrs Johnson?'

'No-o-o-o!' she screamed, plunging the handset down with the full weight of her body, the force cracking the lip of the cradle.

She called the police now, standing in the hall of her new house, quaking. She was finally put through to a female voice who listened to everything she said, making 'uh-huh' noises periodically. When Ann had finished the policewoman tried to reassure her, tried to give her advice over the phone, but Ann was frantic with fear and panic, alone in the house, vulnerable. A uniformed officer was dispatched to calm her down

'And what does he say?' the officer said. 'In what way does he harass you?'

It would sound stupid, she thought, if she told him that all he had said was her name. Her real name. She didn't want the local police to know she was Ann Johnson, christened 'The Neasden Knifer' by the tabloids, the woman who got away with killing her infamous gangland husband in so-called self-defence.

'He makes threats,' she said. 'Sexually explicit threats. He says he will get me.'

'If he ever phones again, let us know straight away.'

'Will you be able to trace the call?' Ann said.

She could see the policeman was thinking about telling her a reassuring lie. 'Just let us know,' he said. 'Meanwhile, take this whistle. It's a referee's whistle. Keep it by your phone and the next time this feller phones you, take a deep breath and give him a blast of that. Then phone me straight away.'

So the following day, when the man phoned, Ann was prepared. Before he could get past his opening 'Hello' she let him have it, full blast. He hung up at once.

As soon as she was sure the line was clear, Ann snatched the handset off the cradle. She listened to the reassuring

18

burr of the dialling tone, then tried to dial 1471. It was hard to do. Her finger was shaking so much she had difficulty hitting the right buttons. She managed it at the third attempt.

The caller had a local telephone number. Her heart sank. She had assumed it would be a London number, a hundred miles away. The fact it was someone local filled her with dread. She wrote the number down, then called the police.

The next day, just after eleven as she was sitting down for a coffee, she answered the knock to find the policeman on her doorstep. He looked grim, and for a brief moment she thought he was going to arrest her for something she didn't know she'd done. But instead he told her she needn't worry any more.

'Are you sure?' she said, desperate to believe him.

'Oh yes,' he said, still with that grim look on his face. 'I'm absolutely sure he will never bother you again, Mrs Singleton. You can be certain of that.'

So the next day she went into town with an immeasurable sense of relief. She had her hair done, restyled and recoloured, then went to collect her dry cleaning.

The dry cleaner's shop was in darkness. There was a sign on the door, handwritten in shaky capital letters. DUE TO A FAMILY BEREAVEMENT WE WILL BE CLOSED TODAY. APOLOGIES FOR ANY INCONVENIENCE.

There was movement inside, in the darkness. Ann pressed her face to the window, cupping out the light. The woman who had served her on Monday was in there, dressed in black, hanging clothes on the rails. She saw Ann looking in, and came to the door.

'We're closed,' she said in a flat voice.

'I'll come back,' Ann said.

'Dropping off?' the woman said. 'Or just picking up?'

Ann held up her ticket.

'You might as well come in if you're just picking up.'

'Sorry to hear of your loss,' Ann said.

The woman nodded. 'It was his heart,' she said. 'The doctors had warned him. Avoid situations of stress, they said.'

Ann remembered the fat man with the greasy skin, the man whose attitude had reminded her of Harry.

'He was a gentle giant,' the woman sniffed. 'Such a kind, generous man. Who would have made up such things? He would never have done anything like that!'

She let herself go, real big tears. Ann placed a hand on her arm, reassuring her, understanding the release she was feeling as well as the grief.

'It was the shock of it that killed him,' the woman wailed, grateful for the opportunity to let out all that emotion buttoned-up inside her. 'The shock of them policemen, coming round and accusing him of all sorts, just on the say-so of some vindictive . . .'

The woman breathed deep, pulled herself together.

'I'll be all right,' she said.

She checked Ann's ticket through her tears and sorted through the hanging garments, taking down the dresses and the skirts.

'Oh,' she said, stopping to recheck the ticket. 'Oh.'

'Is there a problem?' Ann said.

'I'm sorry,' the woman said. 'We . . . my husband tried to call you, before he . . .' She dabbed a tissue at her eyes, holding it together. 'There's a stain on the jacket, Mrs Johnson. We think it's blood.'

'What?' said Ann, horrified. My name is Ann Singleton, she thought. Ann Singleton.

'We think it's blood,' the woman repeated. 'We needed your permission to use a stronger chemical on it. My husband tried to call you, to ask if it was all right. But he...'

'My – My phone was . . . out of order.'

Ann looked in horror at the book on the counter, the name on the counterfoil, the name she had given last week.

'He tried to call you, Mrs Johnson . . .'

Ann felt a shadow fall upon her, crushing her, pushing its darkness into her brain. She gripped the counter for support.

The woman was looking at her, trying to understand.

'Are you all right, Mrs Johnson?'

Free Agents

O'Neil wondered if he would miss her. He would miss the palpitating thrill he felt whenever she stood by his desk to ask his advice, he was sure of that. He would miss her foreignness, the feminine waft and scent of her. She put him in mind of Salome, with her exotic dresses of diaphanous wraps and those kohl-black eyes of hers. She was always a good worker for all that, steady and reliable, but he often imagined her dancing before him, unwrapping veil after veil.

Earlier, he had divvied out responsibility for her caseload in a series of meetings with the other members of his team. Now, in the same shabby conference room he'd held those meetings, there were tablecloths borrowed from the canteen and little posies of flowers. O'Neil observed the transformation and offered no comment. The women from his team and from the two other teams on his floor were fussing over paper plates and plastic tumblers. They had a couple of the men stack the chairs to make space. Another they'd put in charge of the drinks: bottles of warm white wine and cartons of fruit juice. No whiskey, O'Neil noticed. Foil-covered platters were being laid out. Someone had brought in a portable system, a 'beat box' O'Neil believed was the vernacular, and now they set it beating. With a succession of pings, the sub-continental scent of samosas drifted from the tea-point microwave oven. He would miss that, when she was gone. The scent of the orient. He risked a glance in her direction. Across the acreage of the open-plan office, the young bride-to-be was pretending to be oblivious to O'Neil and to all this activity, appearing to be engrossed in something on her computer screen. She looked serene. Persian, O'Neil believed she was, and as beautiful as all Persian women were. He pitied her for what he understood to be an arranged marriage; he pitied the husband-to-be more for the merry dance he would be led.

In the landing toilets, O'Neil sat in a cubicle to gather his thoughts and polish his spectacles. There would be a speech to be made. He pictured himself, standing before them all in his tweed jacket and his unkempt hair, the remaining colour drained from his sallow face, his voice as thin and unconvincing as his features. He unscrewed the top of the silver-coloured flask he'd fished from his jacket pocket and took a long drink from it. *Where are you, God, now that I need you?* The whiskey warmed him, but the warmth quickly faded. He considered drinking a little more, considered sitting there and finishing the lot. In the end, the remnant of what he supposed was his conscience made him tighten the screwtop and return the flask to his pocket. Yet the hollow dread kept him rooted to the lavatory seat.

'—turned out she wasn't wearing any!'

Voices. Laughter. The just-opened door banging shut. Shoes shuffling on the kerb of the urinal. The sound and smell of two men pissing. O'Neil held his breath.

'It's a pity she's leaving, though.'

'The worst of it is that we'll have to endure another bloody sermon from The Holy Father himself.'

More laughter.

'You know, Bridget reckons he really was a priest or something, before they kicked him out of the Church.'

'Yeah, I heard that, too. But could you imagine it? O'Neil?'

'I can imagine him a priest, right enough. He has that do-gooding, holier-than-thou attitude. But I can't imagine him doing anything wrong. He's too fecking *nice*.'

'Yeah? Well, he must have done something. Else why would they have kicked him out the Church?'

There was a contemplative silence. O'Neil knew who they were: slope-headed young bucks from one of the other teams. Two of Bridget Shorey's all-male entourage of hairy-arsed Neanderthals. He pictured them concentrating hard on putting their ape-cocks away.

'All I'm saying is I'm surprised they let him practise as a social worker if he'd failed the test as a fecking priest.'

They left laughing, without washing their hands, and O'Neil took another shot of whiskey. Ignorant fucking bogmen. He came out of the cubicle and stood at a washbasin, scrubbing his hands in cold water till they were pink. Fucking Bridget bastard Shorey.

As fate would have it, the first person he bumped into when he returned to the floor was Bridget Shorey herself, a plate of sausage rolls in each of her dimpled hands. She was one of those overweight women who considered themselves curvaceous and who wore low-cut tops to the office to show off their bulgeous cleavage. She had dressed up for the occasion in a too-tight black dress, with green beads and scarlet lipgloss. He knew her sort, well enough. How many of the men in her team, he wondered, had sought pleasure in the depths of her capacious bosom?

'Will you say a few words?' she said to him. 'When it comes to the presentation?'

'I will,' he said. 'If I'm asked.'

'Aren't I asking you now?'

He automatically smiled back at her when she smiled at him. He couldn't help himself. He cast his eyes down, to her bosom and to the plates in her hands. The smell of the sausage rolls was tempting, and he took one. It was still warm.

'Will you keep your hands off?' She looked him directly in the eye. 'Until later, at least.'

He laughed because she expected it, but he really wanted to confront her, to ask her what precisely she meant in spreading gossip about him. Instead, here he was engaged in some kind of subtextual flirting with her that left his spirit frozen to a block. She winked knowingly at him, misunderstanding his hesitancy, before sweeping off. The sausage roll he had taken now felt soggy and unpleasant. He dropped it into the nearest wastepaper bin. The palm of his hand was smeared with grease and flaked with pastry.

'There's a group of service users downstairs in the lobby,' someone said, a telephone at her ear. 'They're here for the leaving do.'

'We're not ready yet,' one of the women in the meeting room called out.

'Whose idea was it to invite the clients anyway?'

'She did herself.'

'Then someone will be needing to take down that 'You Don't Have to be Mad to Work Here' poster from the wall before they get here.'

'It was a client that gave it to me.'

'Nevertheless, down it must come or there'll be a hell of a fuss.'

'Does anyone know the policy on giving them wine, by the way?'

O'Neil felt the emptiness inside him expanding like the air in a balloon. He turned back to the toilets to wash the grease from his hands and to try to melt the block in his chest with another shot from his flask. One shot didn't shift it, so he tried with another couple until the flask was drained.

'Is this what you wanted?' he said into the mirror. 'Are you happy now?'

He stood with an ear cocked, waiting for a reply. When none came, he let out a bitter laugh. It was no use pretending. He had no belief in God left in him and, more importantly, God had no belief in O'Neil either. They had each let the other down. Before, God would whisper in O'Neil's head, telling him that he was doing right, helping him to understand the iniquities of the world He had created. But they no longer spoke. There was a rift between them, like the cold silent rift between a newly-divorced couple.

O'Neil pocketed the empty flask and, alone, opened the door to face the congregated guests and make his speech.

'It must be a weak bladder you have.'

It was Bridget Shorey again, empty-handed this time, waiting for him on the landing.

'Are you stalking me, Bridget?'

'Stalking you? Is that the sort of girl you think I am?'

Girl? She was forty if she was a day, nearly as old as O'Neil himself. She was laughing, at least, so O'Neil could get away without saying. She drew closer to him and secretly pressed something into his hand. Silver foil wrapped in green and black paper.

'I thought you might be thankful for a Trebor,' she said, and winked again before moving off.

He stood by the landing window for a while, looking out over the car park and beyond, contemplating his next move. He could walk down the stairs and leave, just like that, but where would he go? And what would be the point, after all? It was himself he would be trying to get away from.

27

Finally, he slipped a white disk into his mouth and went to face them all with mint-scented breath. The bride-to-be had been led into the meeting room, which was beginning to fill with her favourite clients and her colleagues from all floors of the office. She was a popular girl. O'Neil spoke to one of her clients, a man considered to have mental health issues because of the voices in his head. O'Neil had got into trouble in the past for suggesting during a case conference that the man had nothing wrong with him, that hearing voices was a blessing, and for putting forward the idea that the man should stop listening to his quack trick cyclists and speak to his priest instead.

'I'm on the medication now,' the man told him as they queued for a drink. 'There are no more voices in my head, at least.'

'I'm sorry to hear that,' O'Neil said, but it came out louder than he'd intended.

The man looked blankly at him and then moved away.

O'Neil drank a beaker of wine and went for another. He was sure Bridget Shorey was watching him, passing judgement. Well, fuck her, and fuck them all. He hated the lot of them.

'It's good to be among friends,' he said when the time came to make his speech. 'And you have so many friends here today to wish you well in your new life, your new career as a married woman and, eventually, I'm sure, as a mother.'

O'Neil caught the look on the girl's face and he coloured, afraid he had said the wrong thing. He cursed the whiskey he had taken, and wished he could take some more.

'Well, I'll say no more on that subject,' he said, to the accompaniment of cheers.

He took a breath to go on, but Bridget Shorey stepped up with a parcel the size of a four-slice toaster in a box, crimson wrap and primrose bow. O'Neil handed it to the girl and raised his beaker in her honour. When he stepped away to get himself a refill the Shorey woman was beside him.

'You kept it short, at least,' she said.

'They don't want to hear a sermon from me,' he said, fixing her with his eyes.

'That's true enough,' she said, unblinking. 'But isn't this wine shite?'

'I've tasted worse of a Sunday.'

'We could get something decent at O'Malley's. Now we've done our duty we could slip away and leave the young ones to enjoy themselves without us old fogeys looking over their shoulders.'

If he hadn't already finished the whiskey in his flask he would have told her to go fuck herself.

O'Malley's was busy with early evening drinkers, office workers mostly. There were a few empty seats away from the bar, and Bridget found them a table in the corner while O'Neil pushed between two groups of dark-suited stout-drinkers leaning against the counter. He ordered a large Powers and a bottle of house red with two glasses. While the barman was uncorking the bottle, O'Neil knocked back the whiskey and leant against the bar to sneak a look in Bridget's direction. She had arranged herself on the little bench seat, the skirt of her black dress just covering her knees, her ankles together, her wrists crossed on the small round table. He took off his spectacles and polished them. She looked different out of the office. A trick of the light, it would be. Or the Powers.

He pocketed his change and edged back through the crush towards her. No, it was more than just an effect of the subdued lighting in the bar. She looked different because she had applied a new coat of red gloss to her lips, re-pencilled her eyebrows, blushed up her cheeks. The air around her sparkled with the tangy sweetness of freshly sprayed perfume. He stood by the table a moment too long, unable to decide whether to call her bluff and squeeze into the space she had made next to her on the bench seat. In the end, he decided to play safe and take the stool this side of the table.

'Oh,' she said, and O'Neil thought there might be disappointment in her voice. But then she said, 'You bought a whole bottle.'

He poured the wine, feeling unaccountably disappointed himself.

She looked at him over the rim of her glass, took a sip. 'Are you after getting me drunk? A whole bottle!'

They both put their glasses on the table and Bridget stared at her wine, waiting for O'Neil to say something. He should tell her she looked nice, he supposed. He had always thought of her, if he thought of her at all, as a bit of a dumpling. She had a little extra padding, sure enough, but he was no Adonis himself. She would have been a looker ten or twenty years ago, with her dark hair and pale skin, her sea-green eyes. He tried to imagine a younger Bridget, and saw in his mind's eye a naked woman in a hotel room in Sligo.

Niamh McCain.

O'Neil took up his glass and tipped back half its contents. The wine tasted sour after the Powers, and it was less effective against the block in his chest. He drank some more.

'You're a nice man, O'Neil. A very kind man. Considerate. I've always thought that.'

'But?'

'But you drink too much. If I've noticed, others will have.'

'Is that it, Bridget? You've brought me to a bar to tell me I drink too much?'

O'Neil drained his glass and topped them both up, although Bridget had barely touched hers.

'You're so pleasant to everybody,' she said. 'You come across as such a placid man, but you can't hide the truth from me. I'm an expert, after all. I'm trained to spot these things.'

'What things?'

'You have an anger, O'Neil. It's eating away inside you.'

He thought of Niamh McCain and that hotel room in Sligo and the consequences that followed. As he had thought of it every day since.

'They call you 'Father O'Neil', you know. They say you used to be a priest.'

'Who would spread such tales?'

'Would it help to talk about it?'

'I'm not one of your clients, Bridget.'

'You're not. But I consider you to be a friend, and I'm asking you as a friend, so.'

She reached across the little table to where his hand was resting beside his glass. She touched him. Her skin was soft and warm. She left her hand on his for a long time. He was not used to such intimacy. It made him feel light-headed.

'You're lucky to have them call you that,' she said. 'They have a much worse name for me. They call you the holy man, but I'm the whore.'

She released her hold on him and took up her glass. His gaze had fallen on her cleavage, and he looked away now, filled with guilt. He remembered sitting in his parlour, fifteen years ago, with Niamh McCain and her blouse open to the top of her bra.

31

He whispered, 'The woman gave me the fruit of the tree, and I ate.'

'What?'

'I said, it's the nature of men to blame a woman for their own faults.'

He thought of the hotel room in Sligo, waiting for her.

'I wouldn't mind so much, O'Neil, but in my case it's the opposite that's the truth. I've not been with a man since my husband up and left. I've lived the life of a nun these past five years, despite the gossip to the contrary going round the office.' She laughed as she said it. 'Mind you, I'd draw the line at a wimple.'

She adjusted the fabric of her black dress, consciously or otherwise, drawing his attention back to the deep cut of the neckline, the pale swell of her breasts. He imagined what they might feel like under the palm of his hands.

Would you like to touch them, Father?

You shouldn't say such things, Niamh. I'm a man of the cloth and you yourself are a married woman.

I'm married to a beast, Father, as well you know. And I can see you looking. I can see you wondering what it would be like.

Will you button up your blouse?

I wouldn't tell, Father.

'What're you thinking, O'Neil?'

'Ah, nothing.'

He emptied his glass and poured himself a third. Bridget covered the rim of hers with a hand. When he lifted his glass to drink she looked at her watch, and he noticed for the first time that she wore it on her right wrist, rather than the left, and with the face turned inwards. He noticed that its green leather strap coordinated with the row of green market-stall beads around her neck, and matched the hue of her eyes. He noticed how beautifully shaped and manicured her fingernails were, how pale was her skin.

'I have a train to catch,' she said.

'You commute, then?'

'I have a little place on the coast. I thought you knew that? I bought it with the proceeds of my divorce, God help me. You'd like the views, if you were to visit. You can see the sea from my bedroom window and hear the waves breaking on the shore in the quiet of the night.'

O'Neil raised his eyebrows. Then he said, 'I'm happy enough with my flat in the city.'

'I'll be honest with you, O'Neil. It's the company I miss more than anything. I have a cat, but it's not the same. The nights can be long and lonely, and now we have a desert of a weekend stretching ahead of us. You know what I mean, I'm sure. We're two of a kind, you and me.'

'You don't know me at all, Bridget.'

'And you don't know me, O'Neil. But that could change.'

'Are you trying to save me or corrupt me?'

'That'd be up to you.'

She reached towards his hand again but he moved it to go for the bottle. He drained the dregs from it into his glass.

'Shall I get another?'

'I should be going,' she said with a sigh.

'Oh.'

He realised he didn't want her to leave. She was right about the loneliness she described, and about the impending emptiness of the weekend. But it wasn't just that he himself didn't want to go home yet, home to his empty flat. It was more that he wanted to spend longer with Bridget. He was just beginning to have a good time. He had thought they might make a night of it. It was Friday evening, after all. He should take her for a meal

33

somewhere. He should move to the seat beside her and tell her the night is young.

Instead, he said, 'Yes, I suppose you have that journey ahead of you.'

He helped her on with her coat, and waited as she buttoned herself in.

'I'll walk you to the station.'

'You don't have to.'

He shrugged. 'Well, I'm going that way anyway.'

They both knew that wasn't true.

They walked through the dark streets separated by the space of an unsaid understanding. He could take the train with her, if he wanted. There would be catharsis, of a sort, if he went with her tonight. She was right. They were two of a kind. Damaged people in need of someone to help mend them. Two people in search of love, even at their age.

Bridget spoke about trivia to fill the silence between them and O'Neil nodded occasionally. His mind was occupied, though, with Niamh McCain, the way she had led him on, the way she had tempted him with first her unbuttoned blouses and then, after that embarrassing initial fumble, with sin after sin until that night they'd spent in the hotel in Sligo. The first and last time. *You are bone of my bone,* he had said to her as they lay naked on the bed. *Flesh of my flesh.*

Will we run away together, Father?

Don't call me Father.

I can't call you anything else. It's what you are.

It's a terrible thing you're asking of me, Niamh.

I also have a husband, don't forget. We'd both be making sacrifices.

Yes, but to leave the Church... It would be God I'd be turning my back on.

34

We'd have each other, wouldn't we?

They arrived at the station. He would have to buy a ticket if he were to go with her. He wished for the voice in his head to return to help him with his decision, to tell him he was doing the right thing. He hesitated. There was nothing wrong in what he was proposing to do. He was no longer a man of the cloth and Bridget Shorey was no longer a married woman. They were free agents.

There were three minutes left before Bridget's train was due to depart. O'Neil turned to her, about to say something he feared he might regret come the morning, when the memory came into his head of the second time he stayed at the hotel in Sligo: by then he was a disgraced ex-priest, waiting in vain for Naimh McCain to leave her husband and join him in his disgrace. He hesitated again.

'Well, goodnight then, O'Neil.'

She leant towards him and pecked him on the cheek, and then she was gone, hurrying through the closing barrier just in time. He stood watching her in a kind of paralysis.

That was a narrow escape you had there, O'Neil.

'It was,' he said out loud, like a liturgical response that would help him believe.

He could see her disappearing inside the last carriage. He waited. A final whistle blew. He suddenly shivered, as if the yellow lights of the concourse were radiating a wintry chill. There would soon be snow. The voice in his head told him he was doing the right thing, that all would be well. But the voice, he knew now, was his own.

The train slowly pulled out of the station. O'Neil stood and watched the red taillight dwindling into the distance until there was nothing left but emptiness, and the darkness of the night.

Holding Hands with Joni Mitchell

It started with a bank job. My part in the heist would be easy – no risk, no danger – and we agreed we would share the money fifty-fifty. The guy with the gun was the brains of the outfit. He was much older than me, around twenty-five, and had a terrifying tattoo – a gryphon or some other mythical beast – on his left forearm. He was six foot tall and nearly as wide across the shoulders. One of his front teeth was missing, no doubt lost in a violent gang-fight with other Hell's Angels, and he wore his black hair tied back in a vicious pony-tail. He dealt in marijuana and prescription pills and lived in a squat with the getaway driver. The getaway driver was nineteen years old, slim and slinky, with long blonde hair and long blonde legs. She reminded me of Joni Mitchell and I was desperately, achingly, hopelessly in love with her. She was in my blood like Holy Wine.

This happened about forty years ago, when I would have been a seventeen-year-old wannabe hippie. I was a wannabe hippie with short hair, though. I told everyone my haircut was a protest against Eric Clapton splitting up Cream, but that was a lie. The real reason I had short hair was that I had managed to get a job as a cashier at the local bank. Unfortunately, the bank didn't approve of long-haired cashiers. Not if the cashiers were boys, anyway.

I tried to act hip, despite the short hair. I wanted to impress the blonde, even though my chances were pretty much zero – after all, she was shacked up with the local drugs dealer – but a seventeen-year-old in love has to believe the impossible. I would see her, sometimes, walking down the street. She was like an exotic bird, colourful and bright in the drab neighbourhood where we lived. I truly believed she was Like a Flamingo, in the words of the song. I spent my days humming that tune in my head, thinking of her. One fine day, I told myself, I would pluck up the courage to speak to her, to take her hand in mine, to confess my love. But, inside, I knew I would never have the courage.

I didn't even know her name.

Then one not-so-fine day, when I was hurrying home from work dressed in my cheap suit and kipper tie, she waved to me from across the street. It had been raining, I remember, and the air smelt damp and sour. I believe that as she waved the rain clouds parted. I believe at that moment I was bathed in sunlight.

She called across to me. 'You're the bank guy, right?'

'Right,' I said.

I didn't know what else to say. I stood on my side of the street like a dog waiting for a biscuit. I was panting.

'Yeah,' she said. 'Cool.'

I wondered if she was wondering what else to say, too.

'I hate it,' I called, before she could turn and walk away. 'The bank, I mean. It's not what I want to do.'

'No?' She looked around, probably checking no one else was about. No one to see her talking to me. Then she adjusted her multi-coloured poncho and stepped through the puddles towards me. 'What *do* you want to do?'

Up close, I could see the pimples under her make up. She was looking straight at me, blue eyes, arched eyebrows, waiting for me to say something. But I had forgotten the question.

She leaned towards me and took hold of my kipper tie, adjusted the knot, straightened it. I could smell her perfume: jasmine and country gardens and blue sky and sunshine. 'What do you want to do? With your life?'

I was trying to stop panting, trying to keep my tongue from flopping out the side of my mouth. She gave up fiddling with my tie.

'Clyde has a plan,' she said.

'Clyde?'

'Sure. He has a plan, to make a lot of money.' She must have seen the *oh yeah?* way I looked at her. 'Okay, not *make* it, exactly. *Obtain* it. A lot of it. We thought of you. Wondered if you wanted to be in.'

'You—you thought of *me*?'

'Sure.'

She folded her arm around mine and we began walking, back the way I had come, back towards her squat. I felt I was in my own private Heaven, twice as nice as Paradise, walking on the sunshine of adolescent love.

The squat was dark and gloomy: brown wallpaper, nicotine-coloured ceilings, unwashed windows. The kitchen smelt of rancid grease and gone-off milk, and I declined her offer of tea. The front room smelt of moulder and damp dust and Clyde. He was sitting at a battered old darkwood table, rolling a joint and humming a tune. It sounded like a buzz saw in his mouth. He looked up as the two of us floated into the room, still tangled at the arm. I was in fear for my life. His eyes narrowed like a killer's as he regarded me. He drew in a double lungful from his spliff and turned his lips inwards, holding onto that breath, still staring at me. I wanted to get out of there before he murdered me, but I didn't want to leave his girlfriend's side.

'Smoke?' he said, breathing out at last and holding the joint in my direction. I had boasted about smoking dope before but, actually, I never had. I looked at the twisted, slightly conical tube of mind-altering substance. I was terrified of offending him, so I took it.

'Tell him about your plan,' his girlfriend said.

'Is he in?'

'Sure he's in.'

The marijuana burnt my lungs, fizzed through my blood, shuddered into my brain. 'Sure I'm in,' I said.

I handed the joint back. My hand was shaking, and the more I concentrated on keeping it still, the more it shook. He didn't seem to notice. He took the spliff, sucked hard on it, then handed it to his girlfriend. He looked at me with his killer's eyes.

'But can we trust him?' he said.

They both seemed to be scrutinising me, weighing up my trustworthiness. I had short hair and was wearing a suit: how could they not? Joni Mitchell handed me the already half-finished spliff, and I was sure she winked at me. When I put it to my mouth I felt the dampness of it, the joy of her saliva mingling with mine.

'I think we can,' she said.

At least, I *hoped* it was her saliva. I looked at Clyde's rubbery mouth, the missing tooth, the little white slimy stuff at the corners of his lips. He put his hand inside his leather jacket and pulled out a piece of black metal the size of a plumber's wrench. He clattered it down on the table. 'Know what this is?'

It had a long barrel and a grime-encrusted handle. There were flecks of orange-brown rust around the trigger and on the bullet chamber. It looked like something left over from the War, something he must have found in a scrap heap. Or maybe under the floorboards in this old house. I took another drag on the spliff. Something in my head went pop.

'Tell him the plan!' Joni sat at the table, her eyes aflame with excitement.

'Sit down,' he said. I did. 'We thought we would rob the bank. With this.' He held up the revolver. Something fell from it, a tiny screw perhaps. I couldn't help myself. I began to giggle. He took the joint from my hand.

'Clyde doesn't want to hurt anyone. The gun doesn't work. And we've no bullets anyway...'

'Here's the plan: you tell us the best time, the best day, to rob the bank. When the safe is most full. Then I come in and wave this about, give everyone a big scare. I pick on you, tell you to hand over the money. You do it. No one gets hurt.'

I giggled again. He was joking, right? His name had gone to his head. He thought they were Warren Beatty and Faye Dunnaway.

Joni rested her hand over mine, and my heart did a little somersault. 'It's a great plan,' she said. 'I'll be waiting outside in the getaway car. Afterwards, we'll all meet up and split the proceeds, fifty-fifty.'

'Don't you mean thirty-three-and-a-third, thirty-three-and-a-third, thirty-three-and-a-third?' I said, still giggling.

Clyde glared at me. 'Don't get smart,' he said. 'It's fifty-fifty or nothing.'

I thought, *This guy is the brains of the outfit!* Despite everything, I couldn't stop giggling. I already felt part of the gang. I *belonged*. Joni squeezed my hand, and she seemed to light up the room with her refulgent beauty. She squeezed my hand again, encouraging me, sending me a message I couldn't quite work out. I wanted to kiss her.

But Clyde stopped laughing and frowned at me. 'So?'

For one terrible moment I thought the marijuana had enabled him to read my mind. I gasped and pulled my hand free from her grip. 'So?'

'So are you in or out?'

I wasn't sure, but it seemed to me he was being serious. I thought of the heavy-duty security guard at the bank, the panic buttons hidden under every counter, the alarm that would ring instantly in the police station just a block away. His so-called plan was a complete non-starter. I had to laugh.

Clyde laughed, too. 'Does that mean you're in?' he said.

It was the marijuana making me laugh. Inside, my ribs were tightening in terror. He was seriously proposing to rob my bank. I pictured him walking into the bank with his rusty revolver. I pictured the guard wresting him to the floor before he could even say, 'This is a stick-up!' I pictured the alarm bells ringing, the policemen streaming in through the door. I pictured Clyde's girlfriend, sitting outside in the getaway car looking like Joni Mitchell in a jaunty Bonnie Parker beret.

Joni took my hand again, squeezing another signal to me. 'Well?' she said.

I pictured her driving off as soon as the police arrived, her role in the robbery unsuspected. I pictured Clyde in steel handcuffs, being hauled away to spend years behind bars. I pictured the accolade I would receive from the authorities for raising the alarm the instant Clyde walked into the bank. I pictured meeting up with Joni afterwards, just the two of us at the secret rendezvous.

Just the two of us.

I squeezed her hand back, returning her signal. 'Sure,' I said, surprising myself. 'I'm in.'

It was as if someone else had spoken. I was there but I wasn't there, as if I were watching a movie that I was somehow a part of. Everything seemed to be happening around me. I felt a kind of deadness, as if I'd given up trying to swim against the current and now I was resigned to going with the flow. Clyde leaned across the table and

42

punched me on the upper arm. He was being friendly. Joni kissed me, a big wet kiss on the side of my face.

'Sure I'm in,' I said again, grinning.

And so I sat there, holding hands with Joni Mitchell and listening to Clyde Barrow plotting and scheming long into the night, planning a bank job we all knew would never happen, dreaming of riches we all knew we could never obtain.

Matches

Mandy made Kris search everywhere, but he could not find a single match. He did discover an old Swan Vestas box in the cupboard under the sink, which rattled when he shook it, but when he slid open the little cardboard drawer there was nothing inside but a collection of dead, wrinkled seeds.

'Didn't you bring your lighter?' Mandy said. Her pose was judgemental, her knuckles resting on her hips, her head tilted to one side. The genetic code must have been passed down from her mother.

Kris shrugged. He wondered if she'd forgotten the scene they'd had the other week, when she told him they both had to stop smoking now, how it wasn't fair for him to keep lighting up when she couldn't. He didn't say what he was thinking because he didn't want it to turn into an issue.

'I'll go outside, shall I?' he said. 'I'll try and find a couple of sticks we can rub together.'

'Won't they all be wet?' she said.

'I was joking. Of course they'll be wet. *Everything's* fucking wet.'

He turned away from her, but she crossed the kitchen and threw her arms round him. The dank air became warm with her scent.

'There's nothing else for it,' she said. 'We'll just have to spend the whole week in bed.'

'That would hardly be practical.'

He shrugged free of her and went to look again in the larder. Mandy's forced cheeriness irritated him. Or perhaps it was the dark, damp cottage that was depressing his mood. If he turned to face Mandy his mood might lighten, but he kept his back to her.

'We need some matches,' he said. 'How are we going to cook all the food we've bought without matches?'

'We could live on fruit and berries. Fruit and berries and *lurve.*'

She grabbed him again. He could feel her belly, hard against his back. If he pulled away again there would be a row, so he allowed her to nuzzle his neck. Her black wiry hair rustled irritatingly against the side of his face.

'I'll phone the woman,' he said.

'Let's just go to bed.'

He retrieved his mobile phone from the pocket of his jeans. There was no signal. 'I thought you wanted a cup of tea. I thought you wanted a hot bath after the journey.' He slipped the phone back into his pocket.

'I'd rather have *you.*'

At last he turned round. The way she was looking at him, her eyes brimming with adoration, flipped a switch inside him. The darkness lifted. He kissed her for a long time and let her lead him upstairs.

Later, though, after he had washed in ice-cold water, he could feel the darkness seeping into him once again. The woman from the village should have mentioned the need for matches when she explained about the Calor Gas situation. She should have made sure there was an adequate supply in the cottage.

In the bedroom, Mandy was still in bed, lying on her back with the covers up to her armpits, her hands resting on the bulge of her belly. 'Wouldn't it be lovely to live somewhere like this?' she said. 'The perfect place to bring up children.'

'It's too cold,' he said.

'But it's so quiet. So peaceful.'

46

'Apart from the noise from those crows or whatever they are.'

She sat up and gave him one of her disappointed looks.

'I'm going into the village,' he said. 'To get some matches. We'll freeze to death if we can't get the fire going in the living room.'

'Come back to bed,' she said.

'We've got all that food, and no way of cooking it.'

'*Please* come back to bed.'

He walked to the little window. All he could see was trees. 'Why did you tell her I was a civil servant?'

'Who?'

'Who do you think? That nosy cow from the village.'

'But you *are* a civil servant.'

'That's just my day job. That's just what I do for money. It doesn't *define* me.'

'She didn't believe we were married. I told her you were twenty-one but she didn't believe that, either. I wanted her to know we're respectable.'

'You should've told her the truth. You should've told her I was a musician. You should've told her I play guitar in a rock band.' He laughed harshly. 'You should've told her I eat babies and chuck tellies out of fucking hotel windows.'

He heard the bed creak behind him. 'What's wrong, Kris?'

He turned towards her but he refused to look at her. He concentrated instead on the pattern of the wallpaper behind her head. 'I'll tell you what's wrong. You kept calling me 'Christopher' when that woman was here. I don't like being called Christopher and I don't like being called a civil servant. You made out I was a boring pen pusher.'

'There's a baby on the way, Kris. We can't carry on pretending we're something we're not.'

'What's that supposed to mean?'

'It means only kids dream of being pop stars. Grown ups live in the real world.'

Something tightened in his chest. He didn't say anything, just looked away from her at the dark trees swaying outside in the wind.

'We need to talk about this, Kris. Things will be different when the baby is here. There will be three of us to think about. We need to plan for the future.'

'I'm going into the village,' he said.

She lay back, turned onto her side, pulled the covers higher.

Of course, the car wouldn't start. He should have known: it didn't like the wet. Rain tended to get into the engine, splashing up from the road, seeping under the manifold. It was a common fault with these old Minis, but he couldn't afford anything more up-to-date. It would be too small, too, when the baby arrived but there was no way he would be able to trade up to anything bigger. He listened to the engine turning over, listened to the battery being drained by the pointlessness of it. When he climbed out he looked up at the bedroom window, expecting to see Mandy there, but all he saw was the reflection of trees and grey clouds. The idea of going back into the cottage was intolerable to him. He would walk into the village. There was probably a quicker route across country, through the trees, but he would stick to the road. He didn't want to end up lost.

He had been walking for about ten minutes when he came to a fork in the narrow lane. He didn't recognise it. When he and Mandy had followed the woman out of the village they had been driving in the opposite direction. They passed it without noticing. There was no signpost, so he had no clue as to which fork to take. Probably, he decided, both roads led eventually to the village. He opted for the lane with a marginally thicker shelter of trees. The rain was getting heavier, and the darkening day drew in around him. He pulled up the hood of his jacket.

The woods smelt of wet earth and bracken. It was an unfamiliar smell, and it unsettled him. He imagined small animals and other creatures all around him. He was homesick for the certainty of concrete and artificial light and the familiar smells and rhythms of passing traffic. Nothing here was recognizable from their drive out to the cottage. He must have taken the wrong turning back there. He should turn back, but there was a part of him that refused to admit to a mistake. Not only did he keep on in the same direction, he began to run.

A movement in the depths of the forest made him stop. A glimpse of light. Rain fell through the leaves and branches in great dollops, exploding on the tarmac around him, plopping onto the hood of his jacket. He peered into the darkness. There it was again, a light raking through the trees. His breathing was heavy from his running, his pulse throbbing in his ears. He tried to listen. There was a car coming.

Kris stood in the middle of the narrow lane and waved his arms above his head. The headlights, full on, blinded him. For one exhilarating moment he thought the car wouldn't stop in time. But it did, less than a yard from his knees.

'I'm lost,' he called into the light.

There was no reply. The car engine continued to purr. Kris pulled down his hood, to show whoever was in the car that he wasn't a criminal. He held up his hands to show he wasn't armed, they way he would if he were in London.

'I'm lost,' he called again.

'Where are you trying to get to?' said a male voice. It sounded middle-class and middle-aged, refined with a hint of northern burr.

'Civilisation!'

The rain was getting heavier.

'You'd better get in then,' the man said at last.

Outside the glaring beam of the headlights, Kris saw how dark the day had become. Almost nighttime. He climbed into leather upholstery and the thick smell of recently-smoked cigar. The man behind the wheel was about fifty, with tanned skin and coiffured hair. His white, immaculately pressed shirt was open at the neck, and he wore red jeans. Red jeans! His teeth, when he smiled, were perfectly even and as white as his shirt.

'Try not to get the seat too wet,' he said.

Kris moved his back an inch from the leather, then saw the man was laughing at him.

'I'm going as far as Ludlow,' the man said. 'Any good to you?'

'I'm not hitching,' Kris said. 'I just need to get to the village. I need to get some matches.'

The man looked at him sideways. His eyes were remarkably green, the colour of crème de menthe. They reminded Kris of a cat, a cat looking sideways at a birdcage. The man smiled, showing off his teeth again, and pushed the lever into drive.

'They probably sell matches in Ludlow.'

'But then I need to get back,' Kris said. 'My wife is waiting for me.'

The man carried on driving, one-handed. His left arm rested across the back of Kris's seat.

'Bit young to be married, aren't you?'

'If you could drop me in the village, that'd be great.'

The man's arm seemed to slither from the back of Kris's seat as he leaned towards his sat-nav.

'What's the postcode?'

'The postcode?'

'You need to know the postcode. You need to know where you're going, don't you? If you don't know where you're going, how do you expect to ever get there?'

Then the man laughed until he coughed. When he recovered, he patted Kris's knee, his hand lingering a little longer than necessary.

'Don't worry, son. I'm only joking. I know the way.'

He moved his hand and rested it in his own lap. Kris thought he might be touching himself but he did not want to look.

'You must be on holiday,' the man said.

'I'm on my honeymoon.'

'Oh, bad luck!' The man roared. Then he pretended to look sheepish. 'Sorry,' he said. 'Sorry. Don't mind me.'

They reached the fork in the road and the man steered the car round the sharp corner.

'I've been married,' the man said. 'Three times, for my sins.'

He slid his eyes towards Kris as he said this.

'Never my idea, of course. It's always the woman, isn't it? Needing the man to prove his commitment. Needing you to give up your freedom to prove you love her. I never took to it myself, but I persevered. Three times!'

His laugh was beginning to get on Kris's nerves. He looked out the window at the black shapes of passing trees.

'So what do you do?' the man said. 'When you're not on honeymoon, I mean.'

Kris set his jaw. 'I'm a musician,' he said.

'Really?' The man seemed genuinely interested. 'That's a coincidence, isn't it? I'm in the music industry myself. Would I know you?'

Kris shifted in his seat. 'I doubt it.'

The man was waiting for him to go on, his emerald eyes on Kris and not on the road. Kris told him about the band, the rubbish gigs in local clubs, the lack of ambition of the other guys. The man glanced at the road now and then, but his attention was on Kris. He seemed to be thinking.

'What sort of music do you play?'

'We like to think of ourselves as the next generation in the line from the Beatles through the Stone Roses to Oasis.'

The man laughed again. 'Well I never,' he said. Then he said, 'Would you believe it.' He slapped his steering wheel. 'I used to represent them. Not the Beatles, of course. But the Roses and Oasis were both on my books at one time.'

Kris studied the man's face, waiting for him to mock him again, the way he had when he told him not to get his seat too wet. But for once the man was not laughing.

'What instrument do you play?' he said. 'Too much to hope that you're a bassist, I suppose?'

Kris shook his head. 'Rhythm guitar.'

'To be honest,' the man said, 'I'm looking for a bass guitarist. I've got this band on my books and let me tell you they're good. I mean, they're *very* good. I've got them a great recording deal and a world tour lined up for next year. Problem is, the bass guitarist just had a nasty motorbike accident, and now I'm in a fix. The clock's ticking and I'm running out of time. We've got the studio booked for next week and I'm starting to panic.'

Kris said, 'I used to play bass in a Beatles tribute band when I was a kid.'

The man regarded him with those green eyes.

'Do you believe in Destiny, son?'

They reached the first houses of the village. Kris thought about asking the man to drop him here. It was still raining. He sat and thought about what the man had said about Destiny. He thought about the way Destiny had saddled him with Mandy. She was a pretty enough girl, good fun at a party and considerate in bed, but he would never have thought of marrying her. He wouldn't have thought of marrying anyone, to be honest. If the baby hadn't come along to spoil everything he would probably be clubbing in Ibiza with his mates now instead of stuck out here in the middle of nowhere, counting the pennies on a cheap honeymoon before the grind of married life and parenthood kicked in for good.

The man drove slowly through the narrow streets. He said, 'It's good you've played bass guitar before. But more importantly, you've got the right look. These days, the look is as important as the sound.'

Kris twisted the ring on his finger, round and round. 'Problem is, I'm a married man.'

'Happily married?'

'Newly married.'

The man sucked in air through his teeth. Then he said, 'No problem. The wife won't mind. Specially when you're top of the charts and coining in the money.'

Kris considered this, pictured himself on MTV. 'Also, there's a kid on the way.'

The man smiled.

'I thought as much,' he said.

He rested his hand on Kris's knee.

'A young fella like you, you seem too smart to get yourself tied down for no reason.'

'But tied down I am, nevertheless.'

'You're sure the kid's yours?'

Kris stopped to consider the question.

'You can check these things,' the man said. 'Have tests done. A musician can't afford to be tied down by kids, specially if they're not his.'

'I'm pretty sure the kid's mine.'

The man finally moved his hand from Kris's knee.

'Too bad, son. This is a once-in-a-lifetime opportunity. It's a now or never decision. Think about it.'

Kris did think about it. He thought about Mandy and the child she was carrying. He thought about the seedy flat they were renting in Hither Green. He thought of his future life as a cog in a bureaucratic machine, sat for the rest of his working days behind a desk in a faceless government building with nothing to look forward to but a pension. Is that what he wanted? He knew it was what Mandy wanted for him – a good, steady job with prospects and security. He thought of the baby, screaming to be fed. More than just the one, probably. It was a life sentence, with no time off to play in a band or pursue his dreams. His creativity would be crushed. He would be nothing but a husk. He thought of the dead seeds in the Swan Vestas box.

'You haven't even heard me play,' he said.

The man grinned. 'You've got the look, and that's good enough for me.'

Kris thought about what his parents would say when they found out. He thought about what Mandy's parents would say. He tried to think of just one person who would understand and support him.

'I can't do it,' he said. 'I have a responsibility to my family.'

'No less than they have a responsibility to you,' the man said. 'Why must you give up everything for them? What are they giving up for you? Where's the fairness?'

The car splashed to a halt outside the village shop. The glow from the shop window flared in the gloom and its

54

reflection shimmered from the wet pavement. Its yellow light gave everything inside the window a golden hue, here and there glistering through the falling rain into diffracted sparkles. Kris new the effect was a trick of the dark day and wet pavement, the rain and the light, but from here the shop had the appearance of a magical place, an Aladdin's cave full of treasures.

'And now it's decision time,' the man said. 'I need to get some more cigars. When I get back, you must tell me whether you want to join me on the adventure of a lifetime. Or if you just want me drop you off where I found you.'

The man rested his hand on Kris's knee again.

'I'll get your cigars,' Kris said. 'It's the least I can do.'

'Okay,' the man said with a victorious twitch of his lips. 'Get me a pack of Coronas. The best they've got.'

Inside the shop, in contrast to the magical exterior, the light was flat and dull. The stale air smelt of damp clothing and wet shoes. It wasn't even warm. Kris took the phone from his jeans pocket and speed-dialled Mandy's number. He wondered how she would take the news, tried to prepare himself for her arguments. He had forgotten there was no signal at the cottage; he was put straight through to her voicemail. He ended the call without leaving a message. As he pocketed his phone, another idea bloomed in his mind. Suppose he didn't tell her. Suppose he just never went back. She would wait there, in the cold and dark, but she would never see him again. No sooner had the thought entered his head than he felt a wonderful sense of elation. It was as if the heavy burden of Mandy and her baby had been lifted from his shoulders. He already felt light and liberated. He could do whatever he wanted. One day, she would see his picture on the cover of Rolling Stone magazine and realise what she had lost.

The shopkeeper, a small woman in a pinafore, asked if she could help him. He hesitated, looked through the window at the sleek dark car outside. The man was grinning back at him, urging him on. He thought, then, of all his unrealised dreams. He thought of Mandy and the kid. He thought of dead, wrinkled seeds in an old Swan Vestas box.

'Can I help you, dear?' the woman said again.

'Yes, please,' Kris said.

But, away from the man in the car, Kris was less certain. Suppose things didn't work out the way he imagined. Suppose he wasn't good enough to play bass guitar in a proper band. Suppose all his dreams of success came to nothing. It was better to be safe than sorry, his dad always told him. Stick to what you know, son. He thought about his dad and his empty life, laid off work at fifty, rotting away from too many cigarettes and too much booze. He thought of his mum, the life she'd had, manacled to his useless old man, rotting away herself. And he looked again at the dark shape of the car outside and the smiling man waiting inside it.

Here in the shop the woman behind the counter was still waiting, an expectant look on her face. He would be a fool to pass this up. You only lived once. 'I'll have a pack of cigars, please,' he said. 'Coronas. The best you've got.'

A shiver passed through him. The woman placed the pack on the counter and waited. Kris picked it up and unwrapped the cellophane. He took out one of the cigars and held it in his hand, feeling the texture of it, smelling the thick brown aroma of it. It was like something from a different world. He knew then that he couldn't do it. He knew he was too afraid to take the chance. Of course, he would tell himself he was doing the right thing by not going off with the man. He would say his conscience got the better of him. He would call it moral integrity. But whatever he called it, however he dressed it up, he knew the truth was he simply didn't have the courage. In the final analysis, it was easier not to take the risk than to grab the only opportunity he was ever likely to get in his life.

He handed the woman his last ten pound note. 'And I'd better have some matches for myself,' he said, feeling the heaviness returning as he spoke.

The woman placed a yellow and red box on the counter. The chill ran through him again. It was a box of Swan Vestas.

Outside, he knew, the man in the car was still waiting for him.

The Piano Teacher's Husband

Every week, when I call at Hannah's house for my piano lesson, it seems her hallway is painted a different colour. It's as though she is trying to paint over something else. Her life, perhaps. If I were a psychologist, like Hannah's husband, I could probably tell you why she does it. But I'm not.

'Zack!' Hannah answers the door and smiles as though she's surprised to see me, holding on to the latch as she steps back to let me in. Today the hallway is a deep red, far too dark, almost a burgundy. It makes me think of dried blood. There are flecks of burgundy emulsion in her hair still, counterpointing the flecks of grey. I want to kiss her right there, right on the doorstep. I fight it. I'm worried that I'm beginning to develop an erotic Pavlovian response to the smell of newly applied emulsion. That's not normal, is it?

'Go through,' she says, the way I imagine she says it to all her students. She has left the door to the living room open, and I can see a brief glimpse of her normal life. A paperback crime novel on the coffee table, along with some style magazines and last week's Sunday supplements. There's a photograph on the television: Hannah with her husband, an old snap taken on holiday somewhere. They are sitting at a table in some Mediterranean bar, smiling at the stranger holding their camera. Hannah had long dark curly hair then, in the picture. I try not to look too closely at how her husband used to be.

Hannah closes the front door and when I turn to smile at her she is leaning back against it. I study her face, wondering what she is thinking, feeling everything inside me starting to race. Maybe she wants to kiss me right here, too. Then she shifts her weight forward and asks me if I would like a drink of something, the way she does every week. And just like I do every week, I tell her I'll have whatever she is having.

'I'll go and put the kettle on then,' she says.

She waits for me to move on down the hall, towards the back room. As I do I look up the stairwell towards the bedrooms. The deep red paint goes all the way up to the landing. I've learned not to comment, or I would have asked her why she chose such a disturbing colour. I'm pretty sure it's got something to do with her husband, but I couldn't say what exactly.

Whenever she can't sleep at night, she told me once, she gets out of bed and brews herself a cup of green tea and then makes herself busy. Cleaning, polishing, rearranging the furniture, redecorating the hallway. She told me there's a name for it, this behaviour, but I've forgotten it.

'I think you should see someone,' I said. 'Get some professional help.'

She snorted at that, to remind me her husband was a psychologist. 'I don't need any so-called professional help.'

'I think you do,' I persisted. 'I think you need help in dealing with your relationship issues. I think you're in denial.'

'What relationship issues?' she laughed. 'I don't have any relationship issues.'

'That's my point,' I said, feeling hurt. 'You're in denial.'

The room at the back of the house is what Hannah likes to call her music room. There's a battered upright piano placed unobtrusively behind the door. There's also a worn brown leather Chesterfield along the wall to my left, and her husband's double-pedestal desk and chair straight ahead, under the window that looks out over the back garden. And there are books. Rows and rows of them, all hardbacks, from floor to ceiling. Her husband's books. All of them first editions. All of them arranged in anally retentive alphabetical order, by author. It's more like a library with a piano in it than a music room.

I put my shoulder bag on the desk and sit on the Chesterfield, waiting for her to bring the tea, wondering what piece of music she wants me to massacre this week. I have the feeling that something inside my chest is tumbling over and over. (Is it my heart? It could be my heart.) I've been getting this feeling a lot lately.

I can't sit still. I get up and wander about the room, looking out the window, taking the buff folder from my shoulder bag then putting it back again, ambling across to her husband's books, running a finger down the spine of Lawrence's *Lady Chatterley's Lover*.

'What's in the shoulder bag?'

She is standing in the doorway, watching me, a mug of tea in each hand. She doesn't like anyone touching the books, and I slip my hands guiltily into my pockets.

'Nothing,' I say, sounding even more guilty. 'It's just my college stuff.'

She looks at the bag and nods. 'What course are you doing again?'

As though she has forgotten. As though I don't mean more to her than her other students. Why does she pretend like this?

'I'm doing a Masters in pharmacy,' I say.

'Oh yes,' she says, as if she has just remembered.

For a minute I think she's going to say something else, maybe even ask me to open the bag and show her, but she doesn't.

61

'You're looking nice today,' I say. And she does. But it sounds insincere now I've said it. I can feel myself blushing.

'Thank you.' Hannah smiles to herself and puts down the mugs of tea on a pile of sheet music on top of the piano. I can tell she's wondering what I'm up to, but she smiles anyway. 'Why don't you play something?' she says. 'Anything you fancy.'

I laugh. I want to say, *I fancy you!* But instead I just say something dumb. 'Play something?'

'On the piano. You're supposed to be here for piano lessons, after all.'

Her face is a shield. I can't tell if she's being serious or playful, what kind of mood she's in. A couple of weeks ago, for the first time since we started this, I thought I was really getting through to her. I don't think I even tried to play anything. We just sat in here and talked. For the whole two hours, practically. It was nice to just talk, to get to know her a little better. But spending that time together like a normal couple, it made me think things I wouldn't normally contemplate. I became aware of other possibilities.

'You know I can't play,' I say. 'Not properly.'

'You can,' she insists. 'I taught you that thing.'

'I don't think I can remember it,' I say. But I pull out the piano stool and lift the lid from the keys. Hannah walks towards the desk behind me. I hear her opening the window. To enable her nosy neighbours to hear my dreadful efforts at playing, I suppose. It saddens me that she insists on keeping up this pretence, the pretence that the only reason I call every week is for a piano lesson.

'I don't feel like playing,' I say, turning away from the keyboard. 'Let's just talk.'

She is facing me, leaning back with her bottom on the desk, her arms folded. Her face is in shadow, but I can still see her eyes, the way she is looking at me. I think she's incredibly attractive – especially for an older woman – and I start to wish and wish she would let me kiss her, just once. But I know she won't. I know she won't, because of her husband.

'You're not here to talk,' she says. 'Let me hear you play something.'

I look at her, backlit by the afternoon light from the window, and in my chest the tumbling starts up again. I turn away from her, back to the piano, and start to play. I can't remember the thing she taught me so I play something else, something I learned last week.

'Whoa!' she says, crossing the room and placing a hand on my right shoulder. 'I don't recognise that. Who taught you that?'

I shrug, feeling the weight of her hand.

'Have you been going to someone else for lessons?'

I shrug again.

She takes her hand away, offended.

She makes me feel like I've been two-timing her. It makes me smile.

I tell her I need to use her loo and go upstairs. It's so dark, with the deep red paint on the walls, that Hannah has to turn on the landing light for me. The door to the bathroom is closed. I sneak past it and creep into the front bedroom. Hannah's bedroom. Her husband's after-shave and other toiletries are still on the dressing table. His spectacles are lying on the bedside table as though he has just taken them off. As though he were still in here somewhere. Sometimes when I call on Hannah I really think he might still be up here. Invariably it chills my blood to think of him, but today it has the opposite effect. Today it makes me angry. Today I am going to get even.

Last week I stole her husband's briefcase. I had noticed it propped on its edge down the side of his desk, a patina of dust along the top of it. I could tell it hadn't been used for ages. No one would miss it. So I took it. I carried it home hidden in my shoulder bag. It was a bit of a long shot, but I was hoping to find out a little more about him, my principal rival for Hannah's affections. I had fallen hopelessly in love with her, but what chance did I have? I was up against everything they had ever shared in their marriage; their whole history together, their shared experiences, all the uxorial memories.

So I was hoping his briefcase might hold something incriminating, something that would change Hannah's perception of him forever. Some kind of illegal activity, perhaps. Or evidence of an affair: amorous letters from a similarly married colleague, for example. But there was nothing. A couple of draft academic papers and a large quantity of documents noting interviews with his patients. I couldn't even claim he had breached his code of confidentiality, for all his patients were referred to only by their initials. Even me.

'Hannah,' I say now, back downstairs and drinking the tea that has gone cold. 'Would you come out with me? For a meal or something?'

'What?'

'I'd like to take you out for dinner. I wondered about this Saturday?'

She looks at me as though I've slapped her across the face. 'Dinner?'

'Like a normal couple,' I say, regretting it immediately.

'A normal couple?' Her laugh has a derisive edge. 'But we're not a couple, are we?'

Now I'm the one who feels he's been slapped. 'We could be,' I say.

'You're my student,' she says, 'That's all.'

'I thought . . .' I'm not sure how to say this without offending her further. 'The way I feel . . .'

She is standing facing me with her hands on her hips, wearing an expression that is warning me to change the subject. But it's too late.

'I'm in love with you, Hannah,' I blurt, ignoring all the warning signs.

'No!' she says, as though she were reprimanding a child. 'No, you can't be! It's not on!'

I know I'm in danger of ruining everything, but I can't stop now. 'I can't go on like this,' I say. 'You know I don't come here to learn the piano. I only come here to see you. I love you!'

She seems a bit stunned by my outburst. It's clear she had never even considered the possibility that I might have fallen in love with her. She tells me I'm being sentimental, immature. She says I'm young enough to be her son, which isn't true, by the way. Then she starts going on about her husband, as though he really is in the room upstairs, saying she would feel as though it was a complete betrayal. How do I think *he* would feel, she says. How do you think *I* feel? I ask her. She looks surprised at that, as though the idea that I have emotions too has never even entered her head. Then she tells me not to be so immature, to start acting like a grown up.

I should keep quiet then, but I can't. I tell her she's the one who needs to grow up, to face up to reality. I tell her she only married her husband until death they did part. Which it did, because he's dead. Remember? Which means she isn't married any more. Right?

'I think you'd better leave,' she says. 'I want you to go right now.'

And she runs out of the room so I can't see her crying her crocodile tears for *him*. She knows as well as I do that she's only pretending to herself. I know she has the same feelings for me that I have for her. But for some bizarre reason she won't admit it, not even to herself.

Sometimes I think I can never win. I am a living, breathing person. I have my faults, like everyone else. But her husband, her dead husband, has somehow become faultless. In her mind, he seems to have acquired this unblemished perfection simply because he has died. He won't change now, not in her mind. Not unless she finds something incriminating.

I take the briefcase and the buff folder from my bag and open the folder. Inside is a selection of erotic love letters to Hannah's husband, written on lavender-scented paper. They are filled with love poems copied from a library book and references to imaginary trysts in hotel rooms. I wrote them out this morning in my neatest copperplate handwriting and carefully folded them all together. I lift them from the folder now, quickly moving to the bookcase, taking down the Lawrence book. I tuck two of the letters inside the front cover, then replace the book in the wrong position, among the Amis books. The rest of the damning letters go into the briefcase, which I then put back where I found it last week.

Then I slip the buff folder back into my bag and sling the bag over my shoulder. I breathe in deeply as I pass back through the dark hallway, drinking in the pungent scent of emulsion paint I shall always now associate with my love, my Hannah. I'm acting relaxed, but inside I'm speeding.

'Ring me if you ever change your mind,' I call out to her as I open the front door, stepping outside into the fresh air.

One day soon I know she will open his briefcase, or spot that the copy of *Lady Chatterley* is in the wrong place. Then she will find the folded letters, an obscene hidden secret. She will see her husband in a new light then. Oh yes!

Her perception of him will certainly change then. It will destroy all her ridiculously sentimental memories of him once and for all. As far as she is concerned it will kill him off for good. You could say I'll have murdered him twice: once with a poison and once with a poison pen.

And once he is finally and utterly out of the way she will find it so much easier to express her grief. With any luck, she will be totally distraught.

And then there I will be, with a caring shoulder to cry on, to help her make sense of it all.

The Parting Gift

All day long his head had been filled with thoughts of how they used to be. Now, for the first time in weeks, Richard's pulse accelerated at the sound of Sarah's key in the front door. He stopped slicing onions and laid the paring knife on the counter. The succulent aroma of a roasting garlic-spiked leg of lamb filled the hot kitchen. He blotted the damp from his brow on his shirt sleeve and prayed she would not go straight upstairs tonight. He reached for his glass of wine.

He thought of how she once gazed at him, before their budding relationship finally flowered, and how her gaze made his breath catch. She made him feel thirty years younger. He thought of how their blossoming love filled his once-cold heart with a deep warmth, and how that love warmed and revitalised Sarah's own empty life. He imagined again the scent of her skin when it was new and unfamiliar to him, the touch of her hand against his hair, the press of her lips against his. Remembering all this almost brought back the feeling, but not quite.

For he could not drive from his mind the sound of her voice on the phone, begging him to come quickly. But he had insisted on finishing his examination of a young girl's tonsils first, and then there was an emergency case to be seen before he could handover the rest of his day's list to the other practice doctors. The drive to the seaside cottage took nearly half an hour. By the time he got there his patient was already dead.

He swallowed his wine and tried to concentrate on the present. He had laid the dining table with his best cutlery and decorated it with the things he bought in town: the new serviettes, the candles, the posy of flowers. He hoped she would appreciate the effort he had made.

But all she said was, 'What's going on?'

'I thought we should celebrate,' he said.

Her heels clacked towards him on the stone kitchen tiles.

'Celebrate what?'

'I received a letter from Veronica's solicitor this morning. There were court papers in with it. A divorce petition.'

His hands still tingled with the smell of onions, his vision hot and blurry. Sarah hadn't even taken off her coat; she unbuttoned it now. She still took care over what she wore to the office, still looked smart in her business suit with her blonde hair pinned up and her makeup on, still became the attractive woman he had fallen in love with. But she only became that woman during office hours these days. The rest of the time she was careless of her appearance, more like his wife than his wife used to be in the end days.

'This is a red letter day for us,' he said. 'My divorce from Veronica will put a line under the past. It will be a fresh start for you and me.'

Sarah didn't say anything. Richard drank her in, taking pleasure in the way she still appeared to her colleagues at least. Although he had made his own efforts to smarten up today he still felt haggard and unkempt beneath his kitchen apron. He felt much older than his fifty years.

'We need to talk,' she said.

Curls of carrot and potato peel on the worktop before him were already wilting, the sliced vegetables already beginning to discolour. He reached for his glass but it was empty.

'That policeman from the coroner's office came to see me today,' she said.

Richard didn't want to talk about the coroner's officer. He wanted to talk about his impending divorce, the opportunity it would afford them, their future together.

Nevertheless, he said, 'What did he want?'

Sarah seemed reluctant say exactly what the officer wanted. She began talking instead about what she had been doing when she had the phone call to say the man was waiting in reception. She told Richard how busy she was at the office, how the unexpected visit was an inconvenience. Richard wanted her to stop talking. He wanted her to just shut up and take another step to be near him. He wanted her to hold him and ask him how it felt to be sued for divorce, to be branded an adulterer.

'Ray's inquest is likely to be reconvened soon,' she said.

Richard waited. He knew the coroner's officer wouldn't have called at her office just to give her a progress report. There was more she wasn't telling him.

'Is that it?' he said finally.

'He interviewed me again. Under oath.'

'You already made a statement. You were interviewed at the time.'

'He said he was tying up some loose ends.'

'Loose ends?'

Sarah looked at the browning vegetables on the counter.

'He wanted to know how Ray got hold of so many sleeping pills.'

Richard waited. She wouldn't look at him.

'He said he was trying to get the timing of events clear in his mind. What time did I discover Ray had taken the pills, what time did I call you, how long it took for you to get to the cottage. Why it took you so long.'

'I see.'

71

She still wouldn't look at him.
'So what did you tell him?'
'I told him the truth.'
Finally, she raised her eyes. Smeared blue.
'I told him the truth.'

As a doctor, Richard knew all about grief and mourning, and he understood that his depression was a normal, if severe, part of that process. He was displaying the classic symptoms of what Freud called 'melancholia'. Meanwhile, Sarah was getting on with her life with no outward sign of loss. She had a stoicism verging on stolidity. It was Richard who had crumbled. It was Richard who felt the pain and self-loathing; Richard who had become withdrawn and unable to work, isolated from the outside world, afraid even to venture into his back garden. Compared to Sarah he was weak and pathetic; it was no wonder she had grown to despise him. He had become the very thing she had detested in her invalid husband.

The irony was that it should be Ray's death that had made him this way. Why hadn't it affected Sarah in the same way? At the time, she had been shocked by its suddenness. She said it was the fact that Ray had planned it, had come to such a decision without discussing it with her, that upset her most. It distressed her, she said, to think of him making the preparations in secret, disturbed her to think that she should be sleeping innocently in the next bedroom while he was actually swallowing all those pills. She said she couldn't bear to be in the house now. She told him she didn't believe in ghosts but she felt an unmistakable atmosphere in the place that hadn't been there before. She put it on the market within a week of Ray's death.

Four months later it was still on the market with no one even viewing it any more.

'I'd better get on with these onions,' he said.

She was still wearing her coat, still standing an arm's length away from him.

'I'm sorry,' she said.

She turned away from him and clack-clack-clacked out of the kitchen. He watched her walk away. When he cut through the onion the paring knife sliced into the flesh of his palm, and yet there was no pain. He heard her climbing the stairs, off to their bedroom to change out of her work clothes. His blood oozed red and thick. The smell of the meat in the oven turned sharp and sour in the pit of his stomach.

She had come into his surgery, that first time, with her husband. Ray was at the end stage of inoperable pancreatic cancer and he and Sarah had bought a cottage on the coast to see out his last days with a view of the sea. Sarah helped him into the chair at the side of Richard' desk and explained the situation, gently persuading him to accept Ray onto his list despite the difficulties it would cause him. The difficulties. She had meant the practice's adverse epidemiological statistics, the extra soul on the mortality returns. But the difficulties had turned out to be much worse than a simple statistical aberration. The dying patient became a metaphor for his own dying marriage. His wife had already left him by then, gone to stay with their daughter at the other end of the country. In many ways, he could empathise with what Sarah was going through.

He cleaned his wound and dressed it with a large waterproof plaster. Then he opened another bottle of wine. His medical training told him that alcohol was a depressive. It would also affect the efficacy of his

73

medication. He poured himself a large glass of it nevertheless. *Here's to us*. He drank half of it in one go.

Sarah became a regular visitor to the surgery, either accompanying Ray or, more likely, calling in on her husband's behalf. She would talk about the effect his illness was having on her. She never formally registered as one of Richard's patients, thankfully, but he listened to her problems just the same. He could tell she was a good wife to Ray, the perfect carer in his fading health. But she was a woman too, with all the normal needs of a woman.

When the oven timer began beeping he turned it off but left the meat where it was, continuing to cook on the still-hot shelf. He untied his apron and carried his glass and the bottle through to the living room, where he sat on a sofa and switched on the television. He could hear Sarah moving about upstairs, going from room to room. He wondered if she was carrying her things from their bedroom into one of the guest rooms. Why not? They never had guests. None of Richard's friends had visited since Veronica moved out. When he'd suggested to Sarah, less than a month after Ray died, that she move in with him on a temporary basis, she pretended to be surprised, even a little shocked. Just until you sell the cottage, he said. Think how it would look to the outside world, she said. He didn't care about that. He wanted to heal her. She was in pieces over Ray's death and he wanted to be the one to put her back together again.

But she was right to have been wary of the outside world. One of Richard's colleagues at the surgery referred the matter to the General Medical Council. The press scented a scandal. Ray's inquest was adjourned. The coroner decided further investigations were needed.

'What are you watching?'

She was in the doorway, wearing an old navy sweatshirt of his and a pair of grey jogging bottoms. Her face looked washed out without her makeup.

'Nothing.'

She seemed to hesitate, as if stepping over the threshold would represent a major decision.

'What have you done to your hand?'

'Nothing. I cut myself. When I was slicing the onions.'

'You *cut* yourself?'

'It was an accident.'

She stood there, just looking at him.

'Something's burning,' she said.

Then she walked away. He switched the television off and listened. He heard the click and meow of the oven door opening, listened to her taking control. It was what she did. He thought of her phone call on that morning five months ago. He was in his surgery, examining a child's tonsils as she sat on her mother's knee, when the phone on his desk rang. He guessed it must be something out of the ordinary for the receptionist to put a call through while he was with a patient. The moment he heard Sarah's voice he knew it was something momentous, even though she sounded perfectly calm.

'Can you get away?' she said.

'No.'

'Ray just died.'

'I see.'

When he arrived at the cliff-top cottage he was struck by the peacefulness of it all. The garden was just coming into life, daffodils and crocuses in the borders, buds on the shrubs and bushes. There were birds singing in the fresh-leaved trees. Sarah showed him up the narrow stairs to the bedroom at the front. The light was clean and blue from the sea and the sky, a forensic light. It fell on the neatly-made bed and the neatly arranged body lying in it. Ray was on his back, covered to his armpits. His hands were outside the covers, crossed carefully across his front. There was a crust of vomit on his cheek. Next to the bed was a small table upon which, among other things, was a half-empty glass of water and two empty pill bottles. Richard picked up the pill bottles and examined them.

'You'd better call the police,' he said.

The moment his life changed.

She returned to the living room doorway now, still reluctant to cross the threshold. She wore his oven glove on her hand and a frown on her face. Her eyes were on the wine bottle not on him.

'You've ruined it,' she said.

Richard thought about switching the television back on to drown out the sound of her pounding on her computer keyboard upstairs. She hadn't come to join him in the living room. She rarely spent time with him these days, preferring instead to sit alone upstairs, surfing the internet. She never told him what she was searching for and he never asked. He drank another glass of wine and pretended to be angry, preparing for the long evening ahead.

He found her in the spare room, sitting at the computer with her back to him. Her hair was up and he admired the curve of her neck, her skin pale and delicate. He remembered how he loved the intimate smell of that area just below her ear, the warm mingled scent of her skin and Chanel, the silkiness beneath his fingers. He imagined touching her, brushing her neck with his lips. He took a step closer but she heard him approach and turned suddenly.

'You startled me!'

On the screen, beyond her shoulder, he saw pictures of apartment blocks, a city estate agent's logo.

'Is that blood on your shirt?'

'It's from my hand.'

'You're supposed to be a doctor,' she said. She got to her feet. 'You can see that plaster won't stop the bleeding.'

She led him into the bathroom and removed the useless plaster. She washed the wound and dabbed it with Dettol. Then she wrapped his hand in a bandage. Richard watched her as she tended to him. The harsh overhead light made her look older, nearer his age. Her mask had slipped, and she looked suddenly vulnerable. It was her vulnerability, he realised, that made her attractive to him. He wanted more than ever to hold her.

'You're getting blood on me,' she said, her excuse for pushing him away.

'I don't care.'

He held her against him and kissed her. To his surprise, she returned the kiss. He broke off to study her face. She kept her eyes closed. He kissed her again, and he could sense something was changing. The invisible barrier that had developed between them, like a magnetic field, began to weaken. She softened in his arms. He kissed her, and felt her melting into him.

'Let's go to bed,' she whispered in his ear.

Richard slipped into a kind of nirvana. He forgot all about Veronica and all about Ray. He slept. Soon, though, his hand began to throb again, and he opened his eyes. Sarah was by her wardrobe, stepping into her pants. Her face had recomposed into its stolid mask. There was no longer any sign of the softness of earlier. She pulled on her jeans.

'Where are you going?' he said.

'I'm hungry.'

'Let me see if I can rescue dinner.'

She opened her wardrobe and selected one of her jumpers, leaving his sweatshirt crumpled on the floor.

'It's too late,' she said.

He looked at the clock. 21:56.

She seemed to hesitate. Then she bent over her handbag, which she'd left just inside the door. She opened it and took out what looked like a pro-forma.

'I need to ask you a favour,' she said. 'I wondered if you would fill this in for me. It needs to be completed by a professional. Someone trustworthy. They said a doctor would be perfect.'

Richard held the form in both hands. It was printed on a single sheet of heavy A3 paper, folded to make four pages of A4, and had the name and logo of a residential lettings agent on the top of the first page. Beneath that were the words 'Character Reference'. He struggled to understand its significance; he was sure it must be important. The paper was glossy, the form expensively produced, but Richard found it difficult to get the document into focus, hard to concentrate on the pattern of words and boxes printed in clear black ink. He could make no sense of it.

'They make all new applicants take one out,' she said.

He still didn't understand. He examined the form again, concentrating hard. *How long have you known the applicant? In what capacity do you know them?* He turned the page. *Please state whether you would consider them suitable applicants for a tenancy.*

'You're leaving?' he said at last. He had intended his voice to rise in astonishment, but as he spoke he heard his words drop into a tone of resignation.

Sarah did not reply. She must have decided there was nothing more to say.

'But why?' he said.

'This was only a temporary arrangement,' she said. 'And I can't stay here any longer. I decided to rent.'

'You've found somewhere?'

'An apartment in the city. Overlooking the river.'

He looked up from the indecipherable form. She must have been making these arrangements for weeks, surfing accommodation sites on the internet, discussing her requirements with letting agents, making lunchtime appointments to view properties. And never a word to him about it. He again considered becoming angry with her, but he could feel his heart was unwilling to allow it. It would be easy to blame his medication for this flatness, but he knew there was a more prosaic explanation than the Prozac. The truth was, he didn't care that she was going.

'When?' he said.

'They need to take up references,' she said. She had been staring down at the floor, and now when she looked up it was only as far as the form in his hands. 'Apart from that one I also have to provide a reference from work and another from my bank. You'd think I was a criminal.'

Her eyes flickered up to his face as she said that last sentence.

'And you think they would accept a reference from *me*?'

'You've no need to tell them we lived together.'

Past tense.

'That's not what I meant,' he said.

He could tell she had understood that but did not wish to talk about it.

'I've taken a room at the Holiday Inn until the references come through and the tenancy's confirmed.'

'The Holiday Inn?' He wanted to laugh. 'What about your house?'

'I can't go back *there*. If I thought I could go back there then I would never have come *here* in the first place.'

At least, he thought, the pain he felt at her words proved he wasn't completely dead inside. There was some hope remaining.

'I've given up waiting for a buyer,' she said. 'I'm not dropping my asking price, and the present economic situation...'

She trailed off. He could tell she had prepared a speech that she now found she could not deliver. She made a gesture of hopelessness with her hands.

'I just can't stand this any more.'

They sat in the kitchen, eating cheese and crackers and drinking red wine as they waited for her taxi to arrive. He wanted to ask her whether their love-making earlier meant anything, or whether it was simply his consolation prize. He wanted to ask her whether she had simply used him all along, whether he had ever been any more than a simple route out of her marriage with Ray. But he did not ask any of these things. He tried instead to pretend everything was all right.

'I took your advice,' she said. 'Remember you once told me to ask my own GP for sleeping pills. I did. I stored them up.'

'You don't—'

'It was Ray's idea. He wanted to go to Switzerland, to that clinic, but he was afraid I would get into trouble. He thought it would be better to make it look as though I had nothing to do with it. I agreed to do what he wanted, even though I knew what the eventual outcome would be. It's what Ray wanted. He planned everything.'

'Even the part where you slept with me?'

She let that pass.

'Today I told the coroner's officer everything. I told him I was with Ray when he took the pills. I held his hand as he

80

did it. Afterwards, when he passed out, I sat with him. I didn't call you until I was sure he had gone.'

'Did Ray know all along about our afternoons together?'

'Does it matter, now? All you need to know is that the press will have a new story and the time it took you to get to the cottage will no longer be called into question.'

He realised she was crying. In all the time he had known her he had never seen her cry before. He resolved to do nothing. There was a new, vaguely familiar warmth in his belly that he eventually recognised as spite. He was pleased she was crying. Deep inside, he had always felt it was her fault that he was in this position, on the cusp of professional ruin. Now he allowed that feeling to froth to the surface he felt elated, as if he had injected himself with a shot of morphine. He was glad she had found a flat and would be leaving him. He couldn't wait to be free of her.

He took their plates to the kitchen sink and ran hot water over them to clean them. The remains of what they'd had washed away. The night outside was dark, and his reflection looked back at him from the kitchen window. Sarah was like a pale ghost of herself sitting at the table behind him. Richard turned off the tap and left the plates in the sink. The morphine-rush of elation at his freedom was dimming into dull understanding. The story she told the coroner's officer was her parting gift to him.

Sarah was still silently crying. He went to her, hoping she would stand and allow him to hold her, but she remained sitting where she was. He touched her neck, but she ignored his touch. He let his hand drop to his side. He understood now.

She sat where she was and dried her eyes. He sat next to her, but still she ignored him. There was nothing he could say.

She continued to sit and ignore him as, wordless, they both waited for her taxi.

The Book Box

I needed a bolthole until the dust settled, and I knew this was it. Maybe it was the sense of light and space. Maybe it was the fashionable stripped and polished floorboards throughout. Or maybe it was because I had fallen in love at first sight with one of my new landladies.

There were two of them, a blonde and a brunette. They said they had bought the flat as equal partners to get back onto the property ladder, but now they couldn't afford to live here and the credit crunch meant they couldn't afford to sell it. Both divorced, both about my age although the blonde dressed a lot younger. She wore tight-fitting designer jeans and one of those tight, low-necked tops that stop too soon and show off too much muffin-top midriff. In her case, though, the midriff was tanned and flat, and augmented with a greenstone bellybutton stud. In contrast, the brunette was dressed all in black. Next to her friend she looked apple-faced and mumsy.

'What do you think?' said the blonde with a flutter of her false eyelashes.

I wet my lips with the tip of my tongue as I returned her gaze. 'Perfect,' I said.

'It's a six month tenancy. After that you have to move out 'cos we'll be selling, assuming the market has picked up again by then.'

'Six months is fine with me.'

'Good. Do you want to see the bedroom?'

It was at the far end of the hall. The walls were deep pink; the carpet deep-pile burgundy. There were red and purple drapes and curtains, and a matching burgundy throw on the queen-sized bed. I could imagine being bound and gagged in this room, and not in a bad way.

'This used to be *my* bedroom,' said the blonde, her surgically perfect breasts pressing against my arm as we stood in the doorway. The brunette had stayed in the living room, plumping cushions.

'Very nice,' I said. I went to the window and looked out on the traffic. Even with the double-glazing you could hear the thrub of it, the occasional roar of a motorcycle. I stepped away as a cop car went past, blue lights and wailing siren.

'This was *my* bed.' She had parked herself on the edge of it and was running the flat of her hand over the silk and velvet covers. 'Don't mind, do you?'

I didn't mind at all. I was trying to work out whether this was some kind of tease, or if she really did mean what her eyes were saying.

'What about your friend?' I said.

She got up from the bed with a sigh. 'She used to have the room next door. Want to see it? It's full of junk at the moment.'

The bed in the brunette's room had been disassembled and propped against the wall. There were seven or eight large cardboard boxes stacked in the centre of the carpet. Planks of wood and bookshelf fittings were piled beneath the window.

'Do I get a rent reduction for this?' I said. 'Or shall we negotiate a storage charge?'

Her laugh was dismissive. 'I'll make sure Eileen gets rid of it all before you move in.'

I followed her back down the hall. The brunette, Eileen, was in the little kitchen, keeping herself busy rearranging cutlery in the drawer. When she smiled at me the whole place lit up.

'He's very keen,' the blonde said to her in a manner that suggested superiority as well as innuendo.

'I'm more than that,' I said. The kitchen wasn't big enough for the three of us. I had to squeeze between them to look out the window. The garden below was in need of some attention. 'When can I move in?'

'We'll need references,' the brunette said, as if she was apologising to me.

'That's fine,' I said. 'I can get references. But references take time, and I'd like to move in straight away. Today.'

The two women looked at each other. The brunette pulled a face.

'I understand,' I said, looking straight at Eileen. 'You need to be sure I can afford the rent. Check that I'm trustworthy. Trouble is, I just split up with my wife. It's all a mess, and I can't face another night in bed and breakfast.' I took a gamble and pulled out a wad of fifties. I appealed to the blonde. 'Suppose I pay the full six months now, up front and in cash? Would you let me move in today?'

The gamble paid off.

The blonde took the money and brunette handed me some paperwork with a set of keys. I signed everything, and the two of them left me to myself. I watched them from the bedroom window, walking to their separate cars, not talking. When the coast was clear, I went out to the motor I had borrowed from Frank without telling him and unloaded the suitcase and my sports bag. The sports bag was heavy enough, slung over my shoulder, but I needed both hands to haul the case up the stone stairs at the front and into the flat. My arms were shaking like an old geezer's by the time I'd finished.

I had trouble getting the suitcase under the blonde's bed. It was over-stuffed and just too large for the gap. And it was too heavy for me to lift onto the top of the wardrobe. Surprising how much paper can weigh. But I did manage to shove the case under the bed in the end. I found some old books in one of the boxes in the brunette's room and used my initiative. Three textbooks on English Law and a fat John Grisham, a bed leg propped up on each. The suitcase slid under the bed easy enough then. I began to feel more relaxed.

I stood in the kitchen and listened to the news on the radio. It was the top item. A full ten-minute report after the headlines. It was bizarre, hearing them all talk about it. I wanted to call one of the phone-in shows to gloat.

That's when I heard the tapping at my door. The inner door to the flat, I mean. Which meant whoever it was had somehow got past the main front door. It could be one of my neighbours, I thought. Someone from one of the flats upstairs, or maybe the bloke I saw in the window of the basement flat, come to tell me to stop pacing about. But it could also be Frank, tracked me down already and out to get even. I went to my holdall and got my Trusty Friend, tucking it barrel-down under my belt so it nestled reassuringly at the small of my back. Then I opened the door a crack.

'Not disturbing you, I hope,' said my blonde landlady with a low-punch of a pout. She held up the bottle she was holding so I could see the label. *Asti Spumante*. It figured. 'Thought I'd pop back, make sure you were settling in all right. Help you celebrate.'

'Celebrate what?' I said, a little too sharply.

'Duh!' she said as she pushed past me into the flat. She had changed out of her jeans and was wearing a dress that looked a size under what she needed. Red it was, with shoes to match. She didn't seem to care about the damage the heels were doing to the stripped pine floor. She popped the cork while I went in search of wineglasses.

'That's a very big suitcase,' she said after we had made our way to what used to be her bedroom. She nodded at the books propping up the bed. 'Wouldn't it have been easier to unpack it?'

'I'll do it later,' I said.

'Would you like me to help you unpack now?'

'You deaf?' I said. I kissed her on the back of her neck. She didn't object, so I kissed her lower and lower as I unzipped the dress.

The bed wobbled and rolled on the brunette's books, but it never quite collapsed. It came close, though. Afterwards, I sat up and rolled myself a smoke. I was the King of the World. Outside, the cop cars went up and down.

The blonde wrapped a thin arm around me and said, 'So, International Man of Mystery. Why did you split up with your wife?'

'What wife?' I said, and sucked on my smoke. She moved her arm away. I said, 'Does your pal Eileen know you're here?'

'God, no! She would kill me if she found out. She'd probably like to kill me anyway. The feeling's mutual.'

'I thought you two were best mates.'

'Used to be. Before we bought this place together.'

I knew exactly what she meant. I once shared a cell with a bloke I'd been to school with. We used to get on okay before, best mates when we were kids, but two months in we were ready to throttle each other. I didn't tell the blonde that, though. She was running her fingers over the barrel of my gun.

She said, 'Now I wish Eileen would drop dead.'

'You should be careful what you wish for.'

'If one of us dies, the other one inherits their half of this place. And the insurance pays off the mortgage. No worries about negative equity then. I'd be free.'

'Yeah? And what would happen to me? I only just moved in.'

'Oh, I don't expect you'll be staying long, one way or another.'

I didn't sleep that night. After she had gone I paced up and down, wishing I could go out for a drink. I thought about my suitcase, under the blonde's bed, and what was in it. I thought about Frank. I thought about the cops. More than anything, I thought about the way I was feeling about my landlady. Love at first sight is madness. It scrambles your brains. Makes you contemplate crazy things.

I stood in the dark, watching the world pass by my window.

Some time after eight the next morning my door buzzer buzzed. I was sitting cross-legged on the floor in the brunette's room, surrounded by the books I had unloaded from her packing cases. The buzzer buzzed again and I went in search of my Trusty Friend.

'They've moved away,' I said into the telephone security system.

'It's me,' said my landlady's voice. 'May I come in? Are you decent?'

The blonde wouldn't have asked.

Eileen was dressed in black again. A smart business suit this time. 'I'm sorry to call so early. I was on my way to work...'

She sat demurely on the sofa she was renting to me, knees pressed together, hands folded in her lap. Pale blue-grey eyes looked up at me. (What colour were the blonde's eyes? I hadn't noticed, and that made me feel bad.) Eileen hesitated, as if she was embarrassed to broach a sensitive subject.

I said, 'If it's about your stuff in your old bedroom, don't worry about it. Shift it whenever, or just leave it if you want. No problem. To be honest, I was looking through your books. Not what I was expecting. Chandler, Hammett, Highsmith. All the greats.'

'I didn't come about that,' she said. 'I came about this.'

She had taken a wad of money from her handbag. Her share of the fifties I had given them yesterday afternoon.

'Oh,' I said.

'Do you think I don't watch the news? Do you think I don't read newspapers? This money is a paper trail that leads straight back to you.'

'Oh,' I said again.

'I'm surprised Julie hasn't been round already, trying to wheedle the rest of it out of you with her charms.'

I decided not to tell her about last night. I decided not to tell her Julie wanted her dead, and that she was trying to steer me towards doing it.

'If you were my client,' Eileen went on, 'I would have to advise you to give yourself up, hand over the money and turn Queen's Evidence.' Then her face blossomed into an unexpected smile, and her bright eyes sparkled like the glistening of morning dew. 'As you are not my client, however, I'll just tell you to be on your guard. Julie is dumb enough to try to spend your hot money, but she's also savvy enough to come looking for more when she finds out it's hot.'

She smiled at me again as she stood up to leave. She had a nice face when she smiled. It was like an open book. I could read every line, and I liked what I read.

'I've arranged for a courier to come and collect my stuff this morning and put it into storage. But if I were you, honey, I'd be long gone by then. Ciao.'

I knew she was right about the blonde, Julie. She was trouble, and she would lead bad luck to my door. But what could I do? I was in love.

The next hour or so I was in a cold sweat, making crazy plans, waiting for the next caller. The police? Frank, come to settle the score? I kept myself busy, repacking the brunette's boxes for the courier and planning my next move. I wanted to call the brunette to thank her for the tip off, wishing I could have had more time to get to know her. I left her a note instead.

I'd made my decision and I had to run with it. Was it love? Or just madness? I had no idea. But I knew there was no one else in my pitiful life I could trust, so I figured I had nothing to lose. I called Julie on the mobile number she had given me, told her I needed to see her straight away. She turned up just as I was preparing to cart the suitcase back to Frank's car. She didn't bother knocking, just came barging in, flashing her long legs and her uplifted cleavage.

'Not leaving already?' she pouted.

'No choice,' I said. 'I made a mistake. I need to keep on the move.'

She seemed to agree. 'You're in all the papers.'

I stopped what I was doing. 'Listen, Julie. How do you fancy coming with me?'

She laughed, but it was false as everything else about her. 'You serious? Where to?'

'Who knows? I know I won't get far alone.' I slung the sports bag over my shoulder. 'Is your car outside? Will my suitcase fit in your boot?'

We managed it, and I could see she was already miles ahead of me.

'You want me to be your decoy, I suppose.'

I took out my biro and wrote an address on the back of her hand. A place I know just outside Calais.

'I'm relying on you,' I said. 'I need you to drive to Dover, get on a ferry. The police'll be looking out for me, not you, so you shouldn't have any trouble getting across the Channel. I'll meet you at this place tomorrow. Okay?'

She tried to look at me as if she was in shock, but her lips twitched up at the edges. Her eyes, I noticed now, were green and full of something I couldn't quite describe.

'Okay,' she said, and leant forward to give me the Judas kiss. 'You can rely on me.'

'I hope so,' I said.

And that, of course, was the last I ever saw of my blonde landlady. Or the suitcase and sports bag I had given her.

I live in Dublin now. A quiet life, it is, on the south side of town. I heard Frank and the rest of them got caught, sent down for a long stretch. But most of the money was never found. Two, three million, they reckon.

I often think of the blonde. I can still picture her face. I can just imagine the look on it when she forced open my suitcase and my sports bag and found they were full, not of stolen money, but of a boxful of the brunette's old books.

Can you imagine?

I had a nice letter the other day from the brunette. She'd kept the note I left her. She says she will be coming to visit me soon, to see how she might like life on the Liffey. Her boxes are still safely in storage. Once the flat is finally sold, she says she might move out here, too. Ship over all her stuff. All her boxes. That's when we'll divvy up the contents of her book box and decide on our future. Together, I hope.

I knew I could trust her.

Like I said, it was love at first sight.

Straw

Her therapist asks her to tell him what she dreams. He is sitting opposite her in the consulting room. His pose is attentive, legs crossed, both his elbows resting on one knee. As she speaks he slowly strokes his beard.

'I'm in a wood,' she says. 'I'm surrounded by trees with high branches. I'm walking between the trees and their arms are waving—'

'Arms?' he says.

'What?'

'You said, 'Their arms are waving'. What arms?'

'The branches. I meant the branches are waving. They are like arms. It's dark. I realise the trees are watching me. They have eyes. They're like the trees in The Wizard of Oz.'

'You remember The Wizard of Oz?'

'Apparently.'

'Okay. What else?'

'What else in my dream? Or what else in The Wizard of Oz?'

'No, what else can you remember about your life?'

'Nothing. I can't remember anything else.'

He sits looking at her, stroking his beard. 'You can't remember anything about your life?'

'No.'

'How does that make you feel?'

'Oh, for Heaven's sake!' she says.

It is night time. She is driving home in the dark from her umpteenth therapy session. She can still remember how to drive. She can even remember most of the Highway Code.

She visualises the route home as a roadmap: blue for the motorway, yellow for the A-roads, red for the B-roads. She avoids the B-roads. She drives the long way round, keeping to the A-roads.

Follow the yellow brick road.

There's a man up ahead, an elderly tramp on the grass verge. Dirty old clothes, battered old hat, wild white hair. He raises his hand to her as she approaches. She slows down. Does she know him? She can't remember.

She stares at him as she passes, but she doesn't stop. She looks in her rear view mirror as she accelerates away up the road.

He is gone.

'There's a scarecrow,' she says.

'In your dream?' says her therapist. 'Or in The Wizard of Oz?'

'In my memory,' she says.

'You can remember a scarecrow?'

'I think so.'

'What does it do?'

'Do? It doesn't do anything. It's a scarecrow. It stands in a field.'

'How does it make you feel?'

'I don't know. What are you talking about?'

'Are you scared?'

She glares at the therapist.

He says, 'Tell me about the field.'

She closes her eyes. She sits without speaking a full minute. Then she says, 'It's just a field. Ploughed. It's on a hill. The scarecrow is on the top of the hill, on the horizon. Blue sky, brown field, black scarecrow.'

'And you. Where are you?'

'I'm at the bottom of the hill. Under the tree.'

'The tree? Which tree?'

She opens her eyes suddenly. 'Let's talk about something else.'

The days are getting longer. As she drives home there is still light in the sky. She thinks about the B-road that runs off to the left up ahead. It leads directly to her village, but it cuts through the woods. She can see the trees in the dusky gloom, a mass of black on the hillside. She slows down, but in the end she sticks to the yellow A-road.

There's a dark figure on the side of the road. It is the old man she saw before. His arm is outstretched. He is trying to hitch a lift. She indicates and draws the car to a halt just beyond him. She opens the passenger window, waiting. If he looks harmless she might give him a lift.

Tick-tock, tick-tock, tick-tock. The indicator counts down her time. She checks the mirror but she cannot see the old man. She turns her head, strains to see anything in the gathering gloom. There's no sign of him. When she turns her head back there is straw scattered on the passenger seat. An icy draught. She shudders and winds up the window. A car horn blares as she accelerates away.

'I know why I'm under the tree,' she says. 'I can remember that much.'

The therapist leans further forward. 'What can you remember?'

'I was in an accident. A car crash. My car hit the tree. I must have skidded, come off the road. I'm trapped in the wreckage. That's why I'm under the tree. I'm trapped in my car.'

'Excellent.'

'Excellent? It doesn't feel excellent.'

'Excellent that you remember, I mean.'

'I can see the scarecrow, up on the hill. It's looking down at me with an evil smile on its face.'

'A smile?'

'Yes. An evil smile.'

'You mean, in your dream?'

'No. This is real.'

The therapist looks at her without expression.

'I know what you're thinking,' she says. 'But he's definitely smiling.'

'Why is he smiling, do you think?'

'Because he's satisfied. Because he's happy that I crashed.'

'I see.'

She notices there are more scarecrows. It must be the time of year, the sowing season, but there are more scarecrows in the fields as she drives home. She is feeling happier than she can remember ever feeling. Her therapist is happy with her too. Remembering the crash is the first step, he told her.

She approaches the junction, the turning off the A-road that leads through the woods. The name of her village is on the signpost. It is ridiculous to keep going the long way round. She has to learn to address her fears. She even begins to indicate. But at the last minute she cannot find the inner strength she needs to face that road, those woods.

And there, just past the turning, is the old man. His arm is outstretched, just like before. She is already indicating. She might as well pull over. She might as well address another of her ridiculous fears.

She stops right beside him, winds down the window. She is petrified. Her ribcage is being battered from within. She can hardly breathe. As the old man lowers his head to speak to her she is fully expecting to find he is really a scarecrow.

'Thank you very much, miss,' he says through the open window. Not a scarecrow at all, but an ordinary old man. 'Thank you very, very much.'

She smiles at him, proud of herself. She has confronted a silly intangible fear. He is an ordinary man. 'Where do you want to go?'

He screws up his face. 'What?'

'Where are you trying to get to? I'm going as far as the bypass.'

'Oh,' he says, grinning in through the window. 'Up the road. I'm just going up the road, miss.'

But there is something about his grin. Something about that row of rotten teeth that fills her with cold dread. When he looks at her she sees a red glint in his black eyes, a glint that wasn't there a second ago. He reaches into the car, his bony hand and uncut fingernails. Straw stuffed up his coat sleeves.

She screams. Stamps her foot on the accelerator. As the car shoots forward the old man is struck by the frame of the car window, dragged forward, thrown to the ground. There is a blaring horn and a terrible crunching sound, metal on metal, and the car jolts to a heart-stopping halt. The other driver is already out of his car, a bullet-headed man, rushing towards her.

'You bloody idiot!'

She is shaking, shaking and gasping, gasping and sobbing.

'You could have killed us both!'

'The – the old man...'

The driver can see she is in shock. 'What old man?'

She dare not look. Her eyes fixed straight ahead, she points towards the grass verge, beside and behind. 'I think I... I think he's...'

The bullet-headed man walks round her car, looks about, sticks his head through the open window.

'What old man?'

'You had a relapse,' her therapist tells her. 'Tell me about the old man.'

She shakes her head.

'You said he was made of straw. Like a scarecrow.'

She says nothing.

Her therapist stands up, paces round the room. Stands behind her. 'You know, some tramps of the Old School, the gentlemen of the road, used to stuff their clothes with straw for extra warmth.'

'It was my imagination,' she says. 'There was no scarecrow. No tramp.'

'You are mixing up your two accidents. There was a tramp before, when your car hit the tree.'

'Was there?'

'Yes. The police found his body in the ditch at the side of the lane.'

'His—his body?'

'Close your eyes and try to relax. Picture yourself driving along the lane. Through the woods.'

'How did he die?'

'That's what I want you to try to remember. Think back.'

'Are you saying I ran him over?'

'Think back.'

She is driving through the woods. He is up ahead, standing at the side of the road, his arm outstretched. She slows and stops, winds down her window.

'Thank you very much, miss,' he says. He is grinning. Those disgusting brown teeth.

'Jump in,' she says. 'I'm going as far as Summerfield.'

'Much obliged, miss.'

She winds down her own window to let in some fresh air. Tries not to breathe in the putrid dark smell of his unwashed body, his filthy rags.

'How far do you want to go?' she says, checking her mirror.

He has not yet closed the car door. Has not fastened his seat belt. His hand is on her thigh. She is taken aback, surprised more than anything. She looks down. His bony hand, his uncut fingernails, running along the hem of her skirt.

'What the hell do you think you're doing?'

He is leaning towards her. The stench of his breath on her face.

'Get out of my car!'

She pushes him away. His chest feels light and brittle, like the breast of a tiny bird. He is undeterred, reaching towards her again.

'All the way, miss,' he says with a leer. 'All the way!'

She pushes him harder. He grins at her. There is spittle drooling from his vile mouth. She seizes the CrookLock from beside her seat. It is cold and heavy in her hand.

'Get out! Get out!'

He lunges towards her. She swings the yellow steel. There is a wet scrunch and a soft moan. She screams, shoves him away, thrusts her foot hard on the accelerator. The old man's body slips from the car. The arms of the tree beckon her.

'He attacked me. I stopped to give him a lift and he tried to... It was self-defence. I panicked, crashed the car.'

99

Her therapist wears a self-satisfied expression. 'The police identified him. He was known to them. A long history of this sort of thing.'

'You knew all along?'

'It was important for you remember. To to come to terms.'

'It was self-defence.'

'No one will be pressing charges.'

She closes her eyes.

'How do you feel?'

'Like I've just got my life back.'

'Excellent.'

The sun is setting as she drives home. An immeasurably heavy weight has been lifted from her. All her memories are tumbling back into place. At the junction, she turns off the main road, heads towards the woods. She no longer has that irrational fear. She begins to sing.

On the hill, in the field above the woods, she can see the scarecrow. It is waving at her. She looks away. There is a horrible dry taste in her mouth. Straw.

As she approaches the woods she has a clear memory of the old man's smell. It is so clear the stench seems almost real. She opens her window. The smell is stronger. She feels the pressure of a hand on her thigh. She looks down. There is straw everywhere. All over her lap, in the well of the seat, floating in the air. She begins to lose control of the car. She looks for the scarecrow on the hill, but it has gone.

'All the way!' he says, grinning at her from the seat beside her. There is a hole in the side of his head where her CrookLock smashed into his brittle skull.

Straw is falling from the wound.

Straw is spilling all over her.

Out of control, the car is accelerating.

'All the way,' the old man says with his evil grin.

Up ahead, the big black tree waits with its arms outstretched.

Declan

I waited in O'Malley's for two hours, but Declan didn't show. So as the big, mock-antique clock struck eight I finished the last of my Guinness and stepped out of Ireland and into the cold April rain of a South London night. It was already dark, and the darkness seemed to be seeping through my jacket, soaking into me with the rain.

'I'll be there by six,' he had said. 'Or seven at the absolute latest. The absolute.' I looked in the direction of the station, away down the hill, but there was no sign. A black chill cut into me, bitter as death. I tried to tell myself he had been held up at the newspaper. Maybe he would phone me later and everything would be all right.

But no one called till 3am. I was asleep on my sofa, fully dressed. I must have dropped off somewhere between my eighth and ninth large Jack Daniels, not that I was counting.

'Harry, were you asleep?' It was Ellie. 'I thought Declan might be with you.'

'No. He's not with me.' I had no right to be angry with her, but I couldn't help myself.

'He said he was meeting you.' She sounded upset, but I didn't care. 'I think he wanted you to forgive us both.'

'He didn't show up. Maybe he knew it would be a waste of time.' The bitterness in my voice didn't seem to register with her.

'He hasn't come home. I'm worried, Harry.'

I tried to sound sympathetic. 'Go to bed, Ellie. Staying up all night worrying about him won't solve anything.'

'Will you come over?'

'That's not a good idea.'

'Please, Harry. I'm no good at being on my own, you know that.'

'Ellie, it's too late.'

That was when she began to cry.

Declan's flat was a ten minute walk away, but it took me half an hour to clean up; to shave, shower and get changed. Outside it was still raining, a gentle drizzle now that helped clear my head of booze. I hadn't been to Declan's flat since Ellie had moved in with him. My footsteps shortened with my breath as I drew near.

The light from their second floor living room outlined Ellie's silhouette at the window, looking out into the night. I waved up at her. She half raised a hand then moved away.

The door to the flat was ajar, but Ellie wasn't there. She had hurried back to the window, keeping her vigil. I closed the door loudly behind me. The hallway smelled different from the last time I was there. More feminine. More like my flat used to smell.

'You took your time,' she said, her back to me.

She was just a girl, vulnerable and frightened. Her thin cotton dress clung to her slim figure, puckering slightly at the small of her back, above the curve of her buttocks. I noticed the way her left hand moved nervously over the soft brown skin of her right upper arm. Her long black hair was loose and wild.

'No news?'

'No.'

I stretched out on the sofa. There were a couple of packing cases open by the TV, filled with her books and assorted knick-knacks.

'Any chance of a drink?'

She turned her head towards me, her expression a knit of concern and annoyance. 'I'll make some tea in a minute.'

I regarded her for a moment, and the thoughts that went through my head made me ashamed of myself. I looked at her the way you would look at something you had once lent to a neighbour and had never had returned. I pulled myself out of the sofa and went into Declan's kitchen to fill the kettle.

'Are you looking forward to moving to America?' I called out, trying to lighten the tone. She ignored me, or didn't hear. I waited for the kettle to boil, and made the tea in silence.

She was still at the window, peering out into the dark night.

'Come and sit down,' I said.

Ellie sat on the floor, cross-legged beside the pine coffee table. She was 24 years old, but she looked much older tonight.

'Do you really want to go to Detroit?'

'I want to go wherever Declan goes.'

I thought about that for a moment. Too many different thoughts raced through my mind.

'He says he'll marry me.'

'You never struck me as the marrying kind of girl.'

'No,' she said. 'It never would have struck you.'

The sound of a car drawing up outside caught her attention, a car door opening and slamming shut. She sprang to her feet. Blue lights flashed outside the window.

The detective who interviewed us in that grey room at the police station was a small man, with thinning hair and pasty skin. I had met DI Trigg before in the course of my work and I knew he was good at his job. I knew I would have to be careful.

'How long have you been living with Mr Fitzgerald, miss?'

'A month, six weeks. I don't know.'

He looked back to me. 'You must have been upset, Harry. Seeing your young lady move in with Mr Fizgerald?'

I shrugged. I wasn't about to let it all out there. Not in front of Trigg, and not in front of Ellie.

'But you remained friends. That's nice. Very mature of both of you.'

'I always knew it was only a matter of time before someone closer to Ellie's own age came along and whisked her off her feet. It just happened to be Declan. I don't blame him.'

Trigg smiled, humouring me. 'When did you first meet him?'

'About a year ago. He wanted me to help him with a story.'

I thought back to that day, in the bar of the Queen's Hotel. He had put me in mind of a farm labourer, the size of him, his unkempt curls, his massive hands with their black-edged fingernails. He bought me a pint and explained that he was a journalist, too. He'd seen a couple of features I'd written on gun crime for the local rag. He said he was doing an in-depth piece for the *Sunday Times* on the local drugs gangs and wanted contacts. At some stage during that extended session I had agreed to get him the information he needed. What harm could it do?

'You introduced him to some dangerous people,' Trigg was saying.

I shrugged.

'What do you know about him?'

'Not much. Late twenties, probably. Nice bloke, if a little misguided. He wouldn't hurt a fly.'

'He hurt *you*.' Trigg nodded in Ellie's direction.

'He didn't take Ellie from me to cause me pain, he did it to make her happy.'

'You liked him?'

I didn't miss the past tense, and wondered whether Ellie had caught it. 'Yes I do,' I said, pointedly.

'So I'm interested in why the two of you were alone together in his flat tonight. Trying to patch things up, were we?'

'Ellie was worried. He hadn't come home.'

'Were *you* worried?'

'Not especially.'

'Not even about what Fitzgerald might think when he walked in to find you alone with his young lady? Or did you know there was no chance he would be coming home tonight?'

'What do you mean?' said Ellie.

I took her hand. 'I think Mr Trigg is about to break some bad news.'

Trigg leant back from the interview table and stroked his jowl. It sounded like the rasp of sandpaper. 'What makes you think that?' he said.

Was this a clumsy attempt to trick me? I wanted to laugh at Trigg's lack of subtlety. Instead, I just said, 'Because Declan's dead, isn't he?'

Ellie pulled her hand away from mine, as though by saying it I had made it happen. Trigg watched her. She looked away from me and up at the high window, the first light of dawn. Her breathing became more obvious, but she was controlling it. She said nothing.

Trigg slipped out of detective mode, and I knew the interview was over. 'I'm very sorry,' he told her.

Ellie sat coldly upright, her hands in her lap, staring at the wall.

'I'll arrange for a car to take you home.'

'I don't want to go back there,' she said without emotion.

'You can stay with me if you like,' I said, feeling Trigg's eyes taking in this little scene.

'Would that be all right?' She wasn't asking me, she was asking Trigg.

'As long as I know where to find you, miss, you can stay wherever you like.'

'Then I'll stay with Harry.'

Trigg looked at me, watching how I reacted, reading my body language, and I knew he hadn't slipped out of detective mode at all.

We slept until lunchtime. When I awoke, it took a moment or two for me to remember that the last few months had happened and that Declan was dead. Despite remembering, it still felt wonderful to be with her again. I kissed her cheek and swept her hair back from her face, then I climbed out of the bed.

I made tea, and was making my way back to the bedroom when the doorbell went. I ignored the ringing and placed the mugs on my bedside table. Ellie was lying on her back, awake, staring upwards. She had been crying. I wanted to say something but the right words wouldn't come.

The doorbell went again.

'It'll be the police,' I said.

She pulled the covers back with a sweep of her arm, suddenly exposing her full nakedness, her skin coffee-brown against my sheets. I swallowed.

'I'm going to take a shower,' she said.

Trigg was wearing the same clothes he had been in the night before, the frayed collar of his shirt unbuttoned, the knot of his plain navy tie low and well off-centre. Another detective, a plain woman with a brunette bob, stood behind him, an inch or two taller. They both needlessly flashed their warrant cards at me.

'Sorry to get you out of bed,' he said. 'This is DS Brown.'

I pulled my dressing gown tighter and ushered them across the hall. Trigg glanced towards the bathroom. The light was on, shining through the frosted panes, and we could hear the whooshing of the shower. He paused for a moment, then walked into the living room and took a seat on the sofa. DS Brown stood by the bookcase, pretending to read the spines. I offered them tea, but Trigg ignored me.

'We've just come from the mortuary,' he said.

I sat on the arm of one of the easy chairs, trying to look relaxed.

'We'll probably need to ask one of you, Miss Gomez probably, to identify the body at some time.'

The body. No longer Declan, just an object.

'Okay,' I said, trying to make it sound casual but not blasé.

'Not a pretty sight, I'm afraid. He was given a thorough going over.'

'They beat him up?'

Trigg stared at me. 'They?'

'Declan was a big man, Inspector. It would take more than one man to have got the better of him.'

I noticed DS Brown had produced a notebook and was writing in it, still standing by the bookcase.

'If you're planning to use what I say as evidence, shouldn't you have cautioned me first?'

Trigg ignored me. 'It seems Fitzgerald may have been tortured.'

He waited, unblinking, for me to say something. I didn't.

Trigg leaned forward, his elbows on his knees. 'Then he was shot through the head.' He made his hand into the shape of a gun, his index and forefinger touching his temple. 'Blam!'

My mouth went dry. There was nothing I could say.

'You've gone very pale,' Trigg said. 'Are you all right?'

I felt fine, I just couldn't say anything.

'Sergeant, get Harry a glass of water.'

I wondered whether this was one of Trigg's little tricks, telling a suspect he looked more affected by the grim details of a death than he actually was. Trying to make me pretend to be upset, so that once I started down the road of pretence it would be so much easier for him to trip me up. He was watching me with those unblinking detective's eyes, looking for subtle indications of my guilt.

'You don't own a handgun, I suppose?' he said.

I snorted in reply.

'I thought not, but we have to ask.'

DS Brown returned and handed me a tumbler of tap water.

'You know I didn't shoot Declan,' I said, but the bitter tone I had intended to use quavered into a guilty-sounding whine.

'As I said, we have to ask.' Trigg nodded towards the bathroom. 'Things have certainly changed for you since Mr Fitzgerald's death, haven't they?'

I didn't say anything. The shower had been turned off but Ellie wasn't coming out.

'So what did Fitzgerald want to discuss with you in O'Malley's last night?'

'I don't know. He didn't turn up.'

'Was it about the girl? You and he fell out over her, didn't you.'

'I thought we'd dealt with that last night.'

'Did we?'

'I think he was going to tell me that he and Ellie were planning to move to the States, but I already knew that. Ellie had already told me.'

Trigg raised his eyebrows. 'So you were still seeing Miss Gomez.'

'No. I bumped into her by chance. A week or so ago. She told me then, quite matter of factly, that Declan had been headhunted by the *Free Press* and they would be moving to Detroit next month.'

'How did you feel about that?'

'What are you? My therapist now? I felt pissed off but when you get to my age lots of things piss you off.'

'You were pissed off when she left you for Fitzgerald?'

'I told you last night, it had been on the cards. I knew it would happen eventually.'

'But you were pissed off all the same.'

'Not enough to kill him, if that's what you're suggesting.'

'Do you know anyone else who would be pissed off enough to kill him?'

'Take your pick. He was writing an exposé on the local gangs. I gave him plenty of contacts. Names of gang members.'

'What names, Harry?'

'Oh, you know, Trigg. The usual suspects.'

'What names, Harry?' He was trying to sound tough. It didn't suit him.

'You know I can't tell you that, Trigg. A journalist never reveals his sources.' That old cliché.

'But one of them probably murdered your friend,' he said, pretending he couldn't comprehend my unreasonable stance.

'I thought you were supposed to be a copper, not my conscience.'

DS Brown suddenly leant forward. 'It might not have been the gangs who killed Fitzgerald,' she said. 'It could have been you.'

I held my breath. She was far more scary than Trigg.

'Was it a disagreement over Miss Gomez? An affair of the heart? Perhaps the whole thing was a crime of passion. When was it you said Miss Gomez told you she was going with Fitzgerald to live in America?'

DS Brown gave me that look cops give you when they know they can fit you up with something unless you cooperate. I felt I was being boxed into a corner, that pretty soon the only thing left for me to do would be to admit everything. I could feel her smugness, her cold sense of victory, radiating out and penetrating right into me.

She waited. Even Trigg seemed to be waiting. But what could I say? That she was right?

Then Trigg laughed. 'Oh, that's a ridiculous idea!'

DS Brown wasn't laughing.

Trigg said, 'She mentioned this theory of hers to me earlier, didn't you DS Brown. I told her then that it was ridiculous.' He leaned towards me, his face close to mine now. 'I said to her, 'You're having a laugh, DS Brown. Harry simply hasn't got the guts.' Have you, Harry?'

Trigg looked at me, then, with utter contempt. Whether it was just another of his tricks, a ruse to provoke me into defending myself by telling him that, yes, I *did* have the guts to do it, I don't know. All I do know is that Trigg succeeded in making me feel utterly weak and worthless and as guilty as sin.

When the cops had gone Ellie said she needed to go home – to Declan's flat she meant – to get a change of clothes. So we walked back there in silence, an arm's length apart, mourning him like a couple of strangers. I watched the faces of the people going past in their cars, counting the number of men who turned their heads to gawp at Ellie. Even in her grief, with no makeup, she was beautiful. In the old days, even before Declan appeared, I knew I would lose her one day, so I prepared myself for it. But when the time came, when Declan came, it was far worse than I had imagined it would be.

There was post on the doormat inside Declan's flat, three pieces of junk mail and an envelope from British Airways.

'It's the tickets for Detroit,' she said, and began to cry again.

I placed a gentle hand on her shoulder.

'Don't,' she said. 'I'll be all right.'

She went into Declan's bedroom and closed the door. When she eventually emerged she had made herself up: mascara and eye shadow, a little rouge, fresh lipstick. She had also changed into jeans and a grey sloppy sweater. She walked past me and stood at the window, just as she had done before, looking out.

'Christ, what am I going to do now?'

'You can stay with me, Ellie. For as long as you want.'

She turned to face me. 'What would people say? What would that policeman think if I move back with you?'

The way she said it, talking about moving back, gave me a little jolt. The possibility of her coming back permanently hadn't occurred to me until then. I liked it that she had assumed that was what I had meant.

'Who cares what Trigg thinks,' I said.

'Won't it look suspicious?'

'So what? I've got nothing to hide.'

She looked at me for a long time, thinking. 'Well, I definitely can't stay here,' she said at last.

So I carried her bag back, resisting the urge to hold her hand or wrap an arm around her, but thinking things might turn out all right after all.

Trigg was waiting for us, sitting with DS Brown on the low wall by the door to my flat.

'Are you moving back in, Miss Gomez?'

I answered for her. 'Temporarily.'

'That's nice,' he said.

I opened the door and Ellie hurried down the steps and, brushing past me, disappeared inside. I heard the bedroom door slam shut.

'I'm sorry, Trigg. She's very fragile at the moment.'

'Oh dear,' he said. 'Will she be all right on her own?'

Something inside me seemed to somehow go upwards and downwards at the same time, a rollercoaster feeling. 'Are you arresting me?'

Trigg smiled. 'Things are moving fast, Harry.'

I could feel the panic surging up inside me, but I forced it back, willed myself to stay calm. Trigg stared at me, his eyes level with my chin. 'You said Fitzgerald was a journalist. With the *Sunday Times*.'

'That's right.'

'He didn't work for the *Sunday Times*, Harry. We checked; they've never heard of him.'

'What?'

'We also checked with the *Detroit Free Press*. They've never heard of Fitzgerald, either.'

'I don't understand, Trigg. What are you saying?'

'I'm saying, Harry, that someone has been lying all along.'

I looked from Trigg to DS Brown to the uniformed officer guarding the door to the interview room. It seemed unfair,

114

all of them and only one of me. It felt as though the odds were against me. And then I realised what I was thinking and stopped myself. It wasn't them against me, I told myself. I was supposed to be on their side. And they were on *my* side. We were all supposed to be working together, trying to find out what had happened to Declan. If I began to think otherwise I knew it would all be up.

'You know, I'm surprised you never mentioned Marcus Gomez was among the names you gave Fitzgerald. Did it slip your memory?'

'I assumed you already knew, Inspector.'

'Did you?'

He gave me that unblinking stare, not smiling now.

'Well, you were right. I do know about Marcus Gomez. In fact, I probably know more about him than you think. For instance, that Miss Gomez's brother is the leader of the biggest gang of drug dealers in South London.'

I didn't say anything.

Trigg leaned back in his chair, which I suppose was some kind of signal for a few seconds later the door opened. A woman, fifty-ish with dyed auburn hair and a pink outfit, walked in. DS Brown gave up her seat for her and went to stand beneath the high window.

'This is Detective Chief Inspector Carson,' Trigg said, not looking at her. 'DCI Carson is with Operation Trident.'

'We concentrate on gun crime in the black community,' DCI Carson said, settling into DS Brown's chair.

'I know what Operation Trident is,' I said. 'I'm a crime reporter.'

'Yes.' She didn't look at me. Her attention was focussed on a small runnel in the tabletop, picking at it with manicured fingernails painted the same shade of pink as her suit. 'I'm afraid the man you knew as Declan Fitzgerald was one of our officers. He was working under cover.'

115

I didn't know what to say to that. I couldn't speak.

'If it's any consolation,' Trigg said, 'we didn't damn well know either.'

'Ah, yes. I'm afraid that was an unfortunate breakdown in communications.'

Trigg snorted.

Carson said, 'You were very helpful, Mr Harriman. You introduced our officer to some very senior figures in the South London drugs scene.'

I said nothing.

'These people trust you reporters. It's one of the reasons we gave our officer the identity of a journalist.'

'Declan,' I said. 'His name was Declan.'

She took a deep breath, let it out slowly through her nose. 'His cover was blown. One of the gangs found out he wasn't Declan Fitzgerald the journalist but a police officer. That's why he was tortured and executed.'

She paused dramatically to allow the horror of it to sink in, but she wasn't as good at this as Trigg. I could see he wasn't impressed either.

'We know who did it but we have no evidence. We need your help.'

'Who do you think did it?' I said, an uncomfortable prickling in my guts.

'We *know* who did it,' she said, looking my directly in the eye. 'Marcus Gomez.'

I felt a rush, a flood of endorphins surging through my body.

'We need evidence,' Carson said. 'We know about your relationship with the Gomez family. We know his sister lives with you.'

I tried not to let the endorphins make me become too confident. I knew I still had to stay sharp. It wasn't over yet.

'If you know all that,' I said, 'then you know his sister won't have anything to do with Marcus.'

Carson looked down at her notes. 'Your friend 'Declan' was building up quite a dossier on Gomez. His sister was *most* helpful in that respect.'

She sat back in her chair, giving me time to think about it.

'So he was just using her?' I said.

'Gomez needed to be brought to justice.'

'And then what would have become of Declan? He would have just disappeared, I suppose?'

'Of course. 'Declan Fitzgerald' would have served his purpose. We arranged a secondment for him with the United States Treasury Department. The Detroit branch of the Bureau of Alcohol, Tobacco and Firearms.'

'So he lied to everyone. He lied to me, he lied to Ellie...'

'Ellie?'

I looked at Carson, the woman who thought she knew everything. 'He was going to take Ellie Gomez to America with him,' I said. 'She thought they were about to start a new life together. He told her he had a job on the *Detroit Free Press*. The bastard!'

She looked flustered at this news, which I could see cheered Trigg up. 'We weren't aware he had any romantic attachment to one of the...'

I began to relax again. I thought she had worked everything out. But I'd forgotten she wasn't as smart as Trigg.

'. . . to Miss Gomez, I mean.' She trailed off, her eyes averted.

Trigg said, 'Don't worry about hurting his feelings, Chief Inspector. Mr Harriman has had the last laugh as far as Miss Gomez is concerned. Haven't you, Harry?'

117

I didn't detect any malice in his words, and if there was any I overlooked it anyway.

'So,' I said. 'Now what?'

DCI Carson said now it was up to me to make sure Declan hadn't died 'in vain'. She set out a simple plan involving some sort of family gathering during which I would be wired for sound and would encourage Marcus to confess all his sins. It was laughable.

'Do I look that stupid?' I said. 'I would be dead within a week.'

'Can you suggest something better?' Carson said.

'Yes,' I said. 'I can suggest you could all just fuck off.'

I caught the smile flickering on Trigg's lips.

It was late when they let me out. I walked back in the sodium-lit darkness, trying to clear my head. I decided to have a quick drink in O'Malley's, for old times' sake. I checked my watch. It was eight o'clock. I stopped outside the pub and looked in the direction of the station, half-expecting to see his farmer's frame climbing the hill. But there was no sign of him, of course, or anyone remotely like Declan.

He had phoned me the day before, out of the blue, wanting to meet to me. I suggested O'Malley's and he agreed. A good choice, he said. He wouldn't say what he wanted to talk about, but I knew it would be his move to Detroit. Maybe (as Ellie had said) he wanted my forgiveness. If only I could ask him to forgive me! Because I'd had a second phone call that day. Ellie's brother, Marcus, called me. He said he needed to get hold of Declan and wanted me to set something up. I could hear the anger in his voice.

I ordered a Guinness now, and sat under the big, mock-antique clock. I had phoned Declan from the call box outside so it couldn't be traced back to my phone. There's been a change of plan, I said. I'm in Brixton. Ah, no problem, he'd said. He would meet me there instead. And then I called Marcus to let him know he was on the way.

I sipped my Guinness, but it went sour in my mouth.

When I got back to the flat, Ellie was sitting in the dark, listening to my old Dawn Penn album on the stereo.

'You've been crying,' I said.

'I didn't think you'd be home. I thought they were going to charge you.'

I held up my arms. 'As you can see, they didn't.'

She rushed up to me and crushed herself against me. I stroked her hair, and she began to shudder.

'What's wrong?'

'I didn't think Marcus would kill him, Harry. I thought...' She was bawling now, uncontrollably.

'Marcus found out Declan wasn't all he appeared to be, Ellie.' I was wondering whether I should tell her what I had found out about Declan today, was wondering how she would take it.

'I know,' she said, sniffling. 'I told him.'

I didn't know what she meant. I wasn't sure *she* knew herself. I held her tighter, told her there was something she should know. Then I said, 'Declan lied to us, Ellie.'

She shook her head like she had a wasp or something tangled in her hair. 'No,' she said. 'Declan never lied to *me*.'

'He told us he was going to be working for the *Detroit Free Press* when you two got to America. That wasn't true. He lied to us.'

'No he didn't,' she said. 'He told *you* that. He told *me* he was going to be working for some federal agency out there, the ATF.'

I stepped away from her. 'You *knew* he was a cop?'

'He didn't lie to me, Harry. When I moved in with him he told me everything. I knew he was out to get Marcus.'

'He told you that?'

'He told me everything.'

She broke down again. I watched her cry, feeling the room shift around me.

'What could I do, Harry?' she sobbed. 'I had no choice.'

'What *did* you do?' I said.

She looked at me, brimming with guilt. 'I told Marcus, Harry! I betrayed Declan, and my brother had him murdered!'

She collapsed into my arms. I breathed in the scent of her hair.

'Oh Harry. What are we going to do?'

'We can't do anything, Ellie, but carry on with our lives as best we can.'

I felt her arms moving around my body. 'I still have two plane tickets for Detroit,' she said.

I kissed her, and she kissed me back. I took her hand and led her towards the bedroom.

Tomorrow would be hell, for both of us, but right now I couldn't bring myself to think about that.

The Second Chance

By the time the police helicopter appeared overhead, its raking shaft of light alerting the whole neighbourhood, it was too late. Susan had already let the guy into the kitchen and was making a cup of tea for him. She felt herself stiffen slightly as the beam suddenly illuminated a large circle of the garden beneath the window, the lush green lawn glistening and sparkling in the searchlight, and she watched as the circle of illumination moved slowly down to the summerhouse where she had first spotted him.

She had been clearing up broken glass when she had sensed an unexpected movement in the dark. She snapped on her torch and there he was, his hood up, crouching by the summerhouse door like a trapped animal.

'Don't move!' she said.

He had been startled at first, as had Susan herself, but then for a moment he seemed about to cry. He was just a boy, after all. No older than eighteen, he was almost young enough to be her son.

'Come here,' she had called. 'It's all right. I won't hurt you.'

But she knew there was an equal chance that he would hurt her. She had to tread carefully. She had to be on her guard, but also reassure him she wouldn't start screaming or dial 999. When she saw he had regained his composure, and rather than run had started walking towards her, it was only her strength of will that prevented her from taking flight herself. But she stood her ground, even as he arrogantly brushed past her into the house. She steadied herself, turned off her torch and followed him into the kitchen.

'Would you like a cup of tea?' she had said with forced congeniality.

Now the helicopter was hovering over the house, searching, scanning the area with infra-red. Relax, she commanded herself. The thudding sound of the helicopter began to diminish as it started moving slowly away towards a neighbouring house. Susan kept her head down, stirring the boy's mug of tea. Then after a deep breath she said aloud: 'It's lucky I found you before they did!'

'Yeah? And who says they're lookin' for me?' the boy blustered somewhere behind her. She was half afraid to turn to face him now, wondering whether he might have a weapon, a knife or something.

'Let me see,' she said, still trying to keep calm, still looking out the window and watching the shaft of light caress the black trees further down and cross the wall into the grounds of the next house. 'First, there's been a spate of burglaries in this area. Second, if they've sent in the helicopter they must think the burglar is on the prowl tonight. Perhaps someone reported seeing something suspicious? And third, I find you sneaking about the garden like a thief in the dark. You can't deny that's more than a little suspicious . . .'

'You accusing me, man?'

She turned away from the window, a determined mask of reassurance on her face, and offered him his mug of tea. 'I hope it's not too strong.'

'You can search me if you like. I ain't stolen nothing!'

He had jumped angrily to his feet and was doing that thing with his hands she had seen rap singers do on TV. He was agitated, volatile. His face was half hidden by his hoody but she could see he was scowling and gnashing his teeth.

She wondered if he was on drugs. Quietly, she placed the mug and the table in front of him and retreated to the kitchen sink.

'I was just passing through, man. Just passing through.'

'I'm not accusing you of anything. I'm sure there's a perfectly innocent explanation for you being in the grounds of a private house at midnight. I'm just saying I bet you would have had a job convincing the police, that's all.'

She had left her handbag on the table and wondered whether she would be able to move it away from him without him noticing. But he caught her looking at it.

'What? You think I'm gonna lift your purse now?' He began to pace backwards and forwards in a little L-shape around the table. 'You people are all the same, jumping to conclusions. Look, man. I was just taking a shortcut, that's all. My girlfriend lives just over there, right, and it's just quicker to cut through here than to stick to the roads. That's the truth!'

'Okay. Okay, calm down.' She was talking to herself as much as to the boy. She pulled off her Marigolds and felt in her jeans pocket for a tissue to dab at her eyes, letting him think she was upset. 'What's your name anyway?'

The boy laughed. 'You think I'm simple?'

'Just trying to be friendly.' Susan wriggled her hands back into the rubber gloves. 'I don't mean to offend you, but I know that not all of us get a fair deal in life. Some people just don't have the privileges the rest of us do. I understand what it must be like in this modern, consumer-driven world, to have less than your neighbour.'

'What you talkin' about? You lost me, man!'

'What I'm saying is, I'm not going to report you to the police. Whatever you've done, or were planning to do, it doesn't matter to me. I believe everyone should be given a second chance.'

123

He eyed her with suspicion.

'To be perfectly frank,' she said, 'I do think you were up to no good out there. That 'just taking a shortcut' line was pathetic!'

The boy stopped pacing and scowled at her. She felt as though she were edging forward in the dark with this boy, feeling her way with him with cautious steps, fully aware that she could step too far at any point and he would explode in rage and violence. But she had to go on, step by step. Fate had presented him to her and she believed in Fate almost as much as she trusted in her instincts. He had been sent for a purpose, she honestly believed that.

'I think you were on the look-out for an empty house you could break into,' she said. 'Am I right?'

He just stared at her, an insolent 'So what?' look on his face.

'I think it's lucky I saw you before the police caught you. I bet you're no stranger to the inside of a police cell, huh? I'd say you know your way around the local Young Offenders Institute pretty well.'

'So?'

He was weakening. Susan began to relax. 'So, the fact that you turned up here, tonight, and I spotted you before the police did, must mean something, don't you think? It's Fate. An opportunity too good to ignore!'

'You some kinda do-gooder?' He finally sat down and picked up the mug of tea.

'I suppose some people would say that. I do my bit.'

He drank his tea, and she picked up a dishcloth, wiping down the counter, polishing up the kettle.

'In fact, I'm on the boards and committees of more than half the charities in the area,' she said. 'But that's another matter altogether. It's not entirely altruistic, I have to admit. I rub shoulders with the great and the good women of the parish on a regular basis.'

The boy snorted. 'Sounds like you only doin' it to hobnob with posh people!'

Susan smiled to herself. 'That's *exactly* why I do it.'

The boy looked puzzled.

'You have no idea what valuable information you can pick up from the boasting wives of the rich. Would you mind giving me a hand carrying some things out to my car?'

Tamely, the boy got back to his feet and lifted one of the plastic sacks Susan had indicated. 'Jeez, what you got in here?'

'I've been having a clear out,' she said, picking up a sack herself and leading him out the backdoor and round to her Mercedes parked at the side of the house. 'Oh yes, charity work can be very rewarding.'

'Nice car!' he said as he heaved the sack into the boot.

'But so expensive to maintain.'

As they returned to the light of the kitchen the boy noticed the broken glass by the door. 'Hey lady,' he said. 'You should get that fixed. Anyone could break in with that window bust like that.'

'You're right,' Susan said, going straight to the table and retrieving her handbag. Before slinging it over her shoulder she unzipped it and pulled out her Walther PPK, her little protector, and pointed it at him. 'Just one last sack.'

'Jeez, lady! Where'd you get a shooter?'

'People can be so careless at these charity committee meetings. They tell you where they're going on holiday, *when* they're going on holiday. They even tell you they use their husbands' birthdays for their burglar alarm codes! How hard is it to find someone's birthday in *Who's Who*?'

'You mean, *you* were burgling this house when I came along?'

'Me? But I'm a pillar of the local community! You're the one with the criminal record, sonny. Oh, and it's your fingerprints all over the kitchen.' She held up her rubber-gloved hand. 'Not mine.'

The boy had put his hands in the air, straight up as though he were doing a stretching exercise, and his eyes were wide with either fear or surprise that this middle-aged lady should be pointing a semi-automatic pistol at his chest. 'Are you gonna shoot me?'

Susan laughed. 'Why should I do that? Like I said, I believe in giving everyone a second chance. But you're going to have to work for it.'

'What do you mean?'

She nodded towards the door into the dining room. 'Go through there,' she said. 'Have a look in the drawers of their sideboard and see whether you can find some table napkins.'

The boy did as he was told, sorting through placemats and coasters until he held up a large square of Indian cotton. 'You mean this?'

'Yes,' said Susan. 'Take two of them and then go and sit in that carver chair. That's the one with the arms.'

Again, the boy did as he was told.

'Now, take one of the napkins and tie your left wrist to the arm of the chair.'

When she was sure he was secure, Susan moved forward and tied his right hand to the other chair arm. Then, to be certain, she took two more napkins and tied an extra bond around each wrist.

'That should hold you for about five minutes or so,' she said. 'Long enough for me to make my escape. I'm afraid I'll also be resetting the alarm, so as soon as you do break free

126

you'll activate the motion sensors. Good luck, sonny. I hope you manage to get out before the police arrive. Watch out for that helicopter.'

The boy didn't struggle. He just looked at her with an even gaze. 'Suppose I just sit here and wait till the cops arrive, and then simply tell them the truth?'

'You think they'll believe you? Kid like you in a place like this? You would still go down for burglary. The cops'll just assume you're covering up for your accomplice.'

'My accomplice?' said the boy. 'What accomplice?'

Susan walked to the kitchen door and paused to switch out the light. 'Don't you guys usually go around in pairs when you go off house robbing?'

He smiled. Too late, from the corner of her eye, she saw a sudden dark movement behind her left shoulder. There was a sharp pain in the base of her neck, darkness and lights shooting up into her head. As she fell forward, dropping the gun so it skidded across the parquet floor, she saw a second boy – the accomplice – stooping down to collect her car keys from her handbag.

'Yes, we do, ma'am,' he said. 'Yes we do.'

Water

The boy could feel his cheeks burning, reddening even more for his being embarrassed in front of his own Nan. She was on her knees, tugging at the hems of his shorts, her warm red knuckles rough against his soft white thighs. As if pulling at his shorts would make them longer! She was cursing him, telling him how difficult it was to get hold of anything these days. Clothes. Shoes. Even a ball of wool if you didn't unpick something. As though growing taller was something he had done deliberately.

That morning she had taken him to the public baths so he would be clean for his trip, even though he had reminded her that he was eleven now, old enough to bathe himself. She had told him to stop being so silly, he didn't have anything she hadn't seen before. She promised to use her sweets coupon to buy him something nice if he behaved.

'Can I have a quarter of Kop Kops?' he'd said, brightening up a little.

'We'll see,' she'd said.

Then she had scrubbed him raw with stinking carbolic soap. Between his legs and everything. She had even washed his hair, and now his ears were full of water, so that he was half deaf.

He tipped his head to one side now, as his Nan continued to tug at his shorts. 'There,' she said thinly through his waterlogged ears. 'That's better.'

Even though the legs of his shorts were as short as ever.

'Let's have a look at you.' Self-consciously he pulled at his frayed shirt cuffs, first the left and then the right, hunching his shoulders to pull his bare wrists up into this sleeves.

She hauled herself to her feet, using the kitchen table for leverage. There was a packet of Players and a box of Swan Vestas, and she took a cigarette and lit it before turning back to examine him.

'I suppose you look presentable enough,' she said, picking flakes of tobacco from her tongue.

He put his finger in his ear and wiggled it about, but the deafness remained.

'I don't want to go to no farm,' he said, trying to sound defiant but hearing his voice through the bathwater in his ears come out in a whine.

His Nan laughed at him. 'You are a one!' she said. She sucked hard on her cigarette, so her cheeks went hollow and the cigarette ash turned bright orange. Blue smoke came out of her nose in two downward jets, like a dragon. 'Shirl!' she called out. 'Shirl! He says he don't want to go now!'

He could hear his Mum coming down the hall from the front room now, her high heels clack-clacking on the lino. He was afraid he might be in trouble, and his throat seemed to tighten, making water come up in his eyes.

'I never said that,' he protested.

The door swung open and he held his breath as he waited for her to appear.

'I can see you,' said his Mum's playful voice. 'I can see you, my little soldier.'

It was a game she used to play with him when he was much smaller, when he would wake up in the night crying. The door to the bedroom would open, and her voice would float in, telling him she was always there, watching over him even though he couldn't see her. It was supposed to reassure him, but it frightened him to think she could

130

become invisible and follow him around. Even when he was in the toilet.

But now he knew she wasn't invisible. She was just looking at him through the crack in the door. *I don't want to be a soldier*, he thought. *I want to be in the navy!*

'Why can't I come on holiday with you, to the Isle of Wight?' the boy said.

He heard his Mum sigh. Now she was cross because he hadn't played the game. He hadn't pretended to believe she was watching over him, like his father the Holy Ghost.

'You just can't,' she said, walking truculently into the kitchen. She was wearing a green frock that rustled when she walked. Her mouth was like a cherry, shiny red and pouting. 'You're *going* on holiday, anyway,' she said. Then she raised her pencilled eyebrows and opened her eyes as wide as she could, as though it was the most exciting thing in the world. 'To a *farm!*'

He had been to a farm before and he hadn't liked it. When he was six he had been evacuated to a cold grey smallholding in North Yorkshire, where it was always damp and he had been always hungry. The children of the family he had been placed with spoke in an accent he could never understand and had bullied him for three years. He hated farms.

'Is his suitcase all packed, then?' his Nan said.

'You'd think he was going for a month!' said his Mum.

'Well then!' His Nan looked at him again, picking a loose thread from his pullover. 'And what about his ration book?'

'Will he need that on a farm, do you think? I thought Dan and me could make better use of it on the Isle of Wight. It's supposed to be our honeymoon, after all.'

His Mum looked around the kitchen until she spotted her handbag on the dresser, then opened it and took out her pack of Kensitas. She lit her cigarette with the American lighter Dan had given her.

'What about my books?' the boy said. 'Did you pack any of my books?'

'Books? How do you think you would be able to carry your case if it was full of books? It's heavy enough as it is!'

'Just a couple, Mum,' he pleaded. 'I can carry them separate. I can put them in my satchel.'

'I said no and I mean it!'

She refused to look at him, staring out the window, trying to blow rings of blue smoke the way Dan had taught her.

'Oh, I'll buy you a comic at the station. A *Beano* or something.'

'A *Beano*?'

His Nan was coughing with laughter, lighting another Players of her own. 'Look at his face, bless him. He can't bear the thought of being without a book!'

'Ideas above himself, that's his trouble. Takes after his father.'

Had his father liked books, then? No one else in his family did. He wanted to ask more, but his Mum would never talk about the boy's father. Not since Dan had turned up.

His Nan kissed him goodbye as he struggled into his duffle coat. She smelled of fag ends and permanent wave solution. Then she went to get his case from the front room as his Mum ran a comb through his hair, digging the teeth deep into his scalp so he squirmed and she had to slap his legs.

'Keep still, you little bugger!'

He knew his Mum didn't like him. That's why she was sending him away to Sussex, to stay on the farm of an uncle he couldn't remember ever meeting before. He was an

132

embarrassment to her and she wanted him out of the way so she could go off with Dan. 'When you come back,' she had said, 'Dan will be your new Dad and we'll be a proper little family.' But the boy didn't want a new Dad. He wanted his old Dad back.

His Mum came with him on the bus to Clapham Junction, and waited on the platform until his train arrived. It was good to be deaf then, the water in his ears dampening the chuffing roar of the engine, the hissing and whooshing of steam. The boy wanted to sit in the compartment that had the picture of the red lion on the door, but his Mum told him all the compartments were the same on the inside and he'd get in the nearest one and be done with it. She didn't kiss him goodbye, but she did ruffle his hair affectionately, the hair she had so painfully combed flat earlier. He knew she was only doing it to show off to the man in the brown suit who was already sitting in the compartment, reading a Daily Sketch. She fluttered her eyelids when the man looked up and winked at her.

'Would you mind putting him off at Hassocks?' she said.

As though he were just a child!

'Of course, love,' the man said, leering.

But half an hour later the man got off at Croydon without even glancing back at him.

Alone in the compartment, the boy wondered why his Mum disliked him so much. He tried to think back to before he was evacuated, before his Dad went off to fight Hitler on the Atlantic convoys. Had she wanted rid of him even then? He couldn't remember. All he could remember was his Dad teaching him how to use a knife to cut string – *Always cut with the blade towards you so you don't accidentally slice your mate* – and how to tie dozens of different knots. Knots were important, he'd said. When you were at sea knots held everything together.

Thinking about the old days made him feel like he was being evacuated again. As though the war was still going on. Just for a moment he felt a surge of panic because his Mum hadn't packed his gas mask. What if he were gassed? He would choke to death, coughing his guts up. She'd be happy then! He acted out his own death in the empty compartment, squirming in agony until he finally collapsed on the bench seat, staring up at the sign above the door.

He released himself – that was allowed if you were playing War on your own – and took out his penknife and a pen from his shorts pocket. He whiled away a few minutes changing the sign to read: Do not **C**lean **S**o**O**t of**F** the window

What was really beginning to worry him was the possibility that the water in his ears had made him permanently deaf. How would he get into the navy if he were deaf? Somehow, he knew this was his Mum's doing. She would do anything to stop him going off to sea. Plus, if his hearing was permanently affected, she could send him away to the deaf school and be rid of him for good. Is that what she wanted? Is that what Dan wanted?

The train finally arrived at Hassocks and the boy got off the train by himself and struggled along the station platform with his cardboard suitcase. A man who smelled of beef stew was waiting for him.

'You've grown, boy,' he said by way of greeting. 'Eh, but you're the image of your cousin Eddie.'

The boy didn't know he had a cousin called Eddie. In fact, there was so much he didn't know. He sat in the cab of his uncle's truck, thinking.

'What's up, boy? Cat got your tongue, eh?'

His aunt turned out to be a large, pink lady with hair like straw. She enveloped him in the suffocating mattress of her bosom, then held him as far back from her as her fat arms

134

would allow. 'My goodness!' she said. 'You can see his father in him, can't you! He's got his father's eyes, that's for sure. And his nose, too!'

The boy wanted to cry. He could feel his ears burning and the water inside them whooshing about.

'Shall I take you up and show you your room? Then when you've unpacked your little suitcase you can come down for some dinner!'

His aunt left him in a tiny room with wooden beams across the ceiling and a small window looking out over green fields. He already missed Putney, and red London busses and growling black taxis. He felt an emptiness in his belly that ached. He sat on the narrow cot bed and opened his suitcase. His clothes were neatly folded, and he was careful not to unfold them as he moved them from the case to the chest of drawers in the corner.

Then, underneath his other pullover, he found a surprise. A red-covered brick of a book with gold embossed lettering on the spine. *Fifty Amazing Adventure Stories for Boys*. Inside the front cover was an inscription: 'Happy reading, pal! Kind regards, Dan.' The boy read the inscription twice, then closed the book and put it on top of the chest of drawers. He bet himself there were no stories about the sea in it. He bet there were no navy adventures.

He took the last of his clothes from the suitcase. There, at the bottom, was another surprise: a little white paper bag. It was a quarter of Kop Kops. Excited, he untwisted the bag and popped a purple-blue sweet into his mouth, sucking off the sugar, waiting for the flavour to go up into his nose. As he sucked at the sweet he felt his right ear pop, and felt a trickle of water run away. Then his left ear popped, too, and he could hear birds twittering outside the farmhouse window.

He could hear again! Now there was no obstacle to his running away to sea, to his joining the navy. How he loved Kop Kops! He wondered whether it had been his Mum or his Nan who had hidden the sweets away for him.

He knew it must have been his Nan.

But he wished it had been his Mum.

The Passenger

The last month of Frank's time inside was hell, but being on the outside was far more stressful. He stood in front of the bathroom mirror, watching himself counting to five as he breathed in, counting as he held it, counting it out. Watching himself trying to relax. He had hung Anna's wet raincoat over the shower-rail, from where it dripped tears of rain into his bath. Her damp dress was draped over the heated towel rack.

'How do I look?' Anna said.

She'd appeared in the doorway, posing in an old *FCUK* t-shirt she must have found in his bedroom. It came down to her knees. He would never wear that t-shirt again, would never wash it. He wanted it to retain the scent of her as a permanent reminder of this moment. She laughed, as if she'd read his mind. He wasn't sure whether it would be appropriate to touch her. They were standing so close, it felt natural to him that he should touch her, perhaps on the arm. But he was afraid of screwing up. They walked together into his living room. She began to wander about the room, examining his things for clues to who he was.

'I'll just get out of these wet things,' he said.

In the bedroom, Frank slung his wet jacket and trousers over a chair near the radiator and pulled on a pair of jeans. He noticed the small indentation on his bed where she must have sat. One of his towels lay damp on the floor. Already the room was beginning to smell different, her light sweetness counterpointing his male muskiness. He closed his eyes, unable to believe his luck, counting in fives.

He left the bedroom and stood for a moment in the little square hall, spying on her through the just-open living room doorway. She was going through his DVD collection.

'What do you think?' he said as he returned to the living room.

'Oh, that's *so* sexy,' she said. 'A man's bare feet under jeans are *such* a turn on.'

He might be a lot of things, but Frank knew he wasn't sexy.

After his first date with Anna, less than a week ago, one of his pals from the old days had commented on Frank's good fortune. Strange, he had said, that this Anna should suddenly take such an intimate interest in him only after his compensation had come through. Frank told his pal to shut his fucking mouth before Frank shut it for him. Calm down, his pal had said. Can't you take a joke?

The so-called joke nagged at him now.

'I'll get the dinner on,' he said. 'Would you like a glass of something?'

'An aperitif would be nice,' she said, looking directly into his eyes. 'Do you have any vodka?'

A few years ago, after everything went to hell, he used to drink a lot of vodka. It didn't help. But his sister, thinking he still drank, bought him a bottle of Black Label when he got out. It was in one of the kitchen cupboards, untouched. But he knew he didn't have any Coke or tonic.

'Straight up with ice is fine,' Anna said when he explained the situation.

He cooked a simple meal: grilled rib-eye steak, baked potato zapped in the microwave then crisped-up in a hot oven, pre-prepared salad in a pack from Sainsbury's. It was quick and easy and looked more impressive than it was, but Frank knew he would have been disappointed if she hadn't complimented him on it. They sat at the small table in the living room, beneath his framed *Double Indemnity* poster. Barbara Stanwyk and Fred MacMurray.

'You're quite a film buff,' Anna said, waiting for him to take his seat.

Frank poured red wine into two glasses. Anna was still nursing her straight vodka. She stirred the ice with her finger and looked at him as she sucked the vodka from her finger. She put down the tumbler and picked up her wine glass. Her pale grey eyes flamed briefly with reflected Burgundy as she drank her wine, still holding him with her gaze. Was it him that she found do suddenly so attractive? Or was it his newfound wealth?

He tried not to think about it. He tried to relax.

'She looks a bit like me,' Anna said as they ate, indicating the poster across the room, the one with Hedy Lamarr from a 1949 sand-and-sandals epic with Victor Mature. It was true. She did look like Hedy Lamarr, the way Hedy Lamarr might look if she had been around today. Anna laughed, throwing back her head to make her hair tumble and shimmer, showing him her throat. Frank imagined being in bed with her, somehow knowing it wouldn't take much to get her there.

'Can I be frank with you?' he said.

'Why not?' she laughed. 'It's your name, after all.'

'I'm a little puzzled. Why are you here?'

She laughed again, but this time it wasn't the same. 'You invited me for dinner.'

'But what made you accept?'

'I like you, Frank. You're a nice man. Gentle.'

Now it was his turn to laugh. No one had ever called him gentle before.

She frowned. 'Are you all right?'

'I'm fine.'

But he wasn't. He emptied his glass and poured himself another.

Anna put her knife and fork down on either side of her plate. All she had eaten so far was salad. 'Do you want me to go?'

'No, of course not,' he said, wondering if maybe he did. Why was he doing this? Why couldn't he just accept that she might really like him? His therapist would probably be able to explain it. He would give it a fancy-sounding name, *parataxic distortion*, probably. His favourite phrase. Meaning every woman he meets doesn't have to be the ghost of his wife.

Anna reached across the table and placed her hands over his, squeezing gently.

'Baggage, eh?' she said.

He didn't understand what she meant, but he set his jaw and made a brave face as if he did.

'It's all right, Frank. I know I'm the first woman you've been out with since you... since your wife died. I can appreciate how tough it must be, getting back into the saddle. But I'm nothing like your wife, okay? I'm me, and I'm here because I want to be here. No other reason.'

It was as if she had read his mind. Frank turned his hands over, palms up, and returned her grip. He really wanted to believe her. 'You know what happened?' he said.

'I know about the court case,' she said. 'It must have been terrible for you. Not just the injustice of it. All the untrue newspaper headlines, too.'

He let go of her hands.

'Can I tell you a secret?' she said. She took up her tumbler, throwing the vodka back in one and reaching now for her wine glass.

'Depends what it is.'

She finished the wine and waited while he refilled their glasses. 'You're the first man I've been out with for some time, Frank. And I wouldn't be here if it wasn't for the fact I really like you.'

'Is that it?' he said. 'Is that your secret?'

'No,' she said, looking somewhere into the distance. 'No, that isn't my secret.'

She stood up and walked away from the table, taking her glass with her. Frank stayed sitting. She made her way to his film collection.

'Don't you have anything modern?'

She selected a DVD and read the back credits. Frank could see from the spine it was *A Streetcar Named Desire*. He waited for her to say something. In the ensuing silence they heard a car slush past outside, slow down and come to a halt nearby. They could hear the engine still running.

'A few years ago I went through a difficult divorce,' she eventually said, looking down at the black and white still of Brando. 'My husband was a complete bastard. Violent. For a long time afterwards, I thought all men were brutes.'

She put the DVD back.

'It has taken me a long time to get over that, but I'm getting there. So I guess we both have baggage to deal with.'

She walked halfway towards him. He got to his feet, unsure whether to go to her. Outside, a car door slammed. There were raised voices.

'Hold me, Frank,' she said. She was shaking perceptibly. He could see tears.

Just as he took her in his arms they heard a shrill scream. They went to the window together, pulled back the curtains, looked out into the dark night. Through the rain-streaked glass they could see a man and a woman under a streetlight. He had grabbed her and she was struggling. His car door was open. She screamed again.

Without thinking it through, Frank ran from the room and out into the street. The tarmac was cold beneath his bare feet, but the rain was surprisingly warm.

'What's going on?' he yelled.

The man holding the woman released his grip, took a step back. His victim looked very young up close, not much more than a girl, but made up to appear a lot older. Her push-up bra was clearly visible through her white blouse, wetly translucent with the rain. Her scarlet skirt barely covered her hips. No tights.

'He tried to... He tried to...' She was gasping for breath, pointing at her attacker.

Frank grabbed the man by the lapels and forced him back against the side of his car. He was a big man, and much younger than Frank. But he didn't want to fight. A typical bully. A typical molester of defenceless girls.

'You filthy bastard,' Frank said. He clenched his fist, red anger coursing through him. Across the street, he could see the light from his window between parted curtains, and Anna's shadowy silhouette.

'Wait!' the man shouted. 'Wait!'

But Frank was too angry to wait. He hit the man hard in the face. The man groaned and slumped to the ground.

'Phone the police,' Frank called over his shoulder, but when he looked the girl had gone. Too frightened to stick around.

'Get to your feet,' he said, dragging the man up from the slick wet pavement.

'She—she wouldn't pay,' he gasped, wiping his bloody lip on the back of his hand.

'You bastard!' said Frank. 'You filthy animal.'

The man flinched. 'Please!' he said. 'I'm not an animal. I'm a minicab driver. This is my minicab. She refused to pay her fare.'

Frank tightened his grip on the man's lapel, but he could see the truth in his eyes.

'I'm going to call the police,' Frank said. 'Let them decide.'

'Yes,' said the man, nodding vigorously. 'Call the police. Don't hit me again.'

Frank let go of the lapels. The two men stood facing each other in the pouring rain. Frank's feet were getting cold.

'Wait here,' he said.

The man got into his minicab. Frank crossed the street. Anna was standing at the door.

'The girl said he attacked her,' Frank said, but Anna turned away and shut herself in the bathroom. Before he had finished his phone call she had changed back into her damp dress. He watched her struggle into her wet raincoat. She left without saying another word to him.

He never saw Anna again. Within a month, her scent had already faded from his unwashed *FCUK* t-shirt.

But Frank did see the passenger again. It was a weekday afternoon. She was wearing a school uniform and was larking about with a group of her friends outside McDonald's. She had forgotten the incident with the cab driver and didn't seem to recognise Frank. But he recognised her all right. He followed her home.

After that, apart from the picture of her in the local newspaper, he never saw the passenger again, either.

The Consequences of Enchantment

Anna was in the middle of putting things straight when she found the key. A customer must have dropped it. It was an ordinary door key, with no keyring. She bent down to pick it up. It was then that she suddenly and intuitively knew she was being watched. She stood at once and adjusted her shift. A man was standing in the doorway, where he had probably stopped to look at the menu in the window, but now his wide eyes were staring directly at her, his jaw heavy and slack. At first, she thought she must know him. He was wearing a hat, a fedora, and a belted raincoat, as if he had just stepped off the set of an old movie. She thought he must be about forty, older than her but not by much. He was staring at her through the glass doors as if he were looking at a ghost. His face put her in mind of Humphrey Bogart, ugly-handsome, lived in. She turned away, collected the plates and empty bottles from the last table. There was a mirror on the far wall and she could see his reflection, standing outside in the shadows and the window-light, staring in at her. She took the plates through to the heat of the kitchen.

'There's a man in the doorway,' she said, trying to sound matter-of-fact.

'Tell him we're closed,' Luigi said. 'Doesn't he know what time it is?'

'You tell him,' she said, and went out the back for some fresh air. It was raining. She still had the key in her hand. She closed her eyes and let the rain fall onto her tongue. It felt like pins of ice but it tasted fresh and sweet.

The man in the doorway was called Michael Roth. He had stepped in to shelter from the rain, and now he waited for the dark-haired waitress to reappear from the kitchen. It was a small restaurant, an old-fashioned Trattoria. Plastic vines hung from the ceiling. Italian tourist posters were plastered over murals of the bay of Naples. Old bottles of Chianti were used as candle-holders on each of the tables. Apart from a middle-aged couple in the corner, the place was empty. Roth waited, unsure what he should do. He felt the way a limb that has grown numb feels when its blood supply is restored. The sudden surge of life-force through him was an agony of prickly rebirth.

Inside the restaurant, a fat man wearing black and white chequered trousers and a white buttoned-up top came from the kitchen and marched towards the door. His round face glistened and the thin strands of his black hair were plastered to his scalp. His hands were huge and red. When he opened the door, Roth could smell heat and garlic.

'I'm sorry, *signore*. We are closed.'

Roth felt suddenly crushed. He looked beyond the chef, looked over his shoulder towards the kitchen, praying for her to come back one last time.

'I said we're closed.'

'That waitress,' Roth said, standing his ground. 'I know her.'

'Really? Then why did she send me out here to tell you to go away?'

Roth looked at him. There was a possessiveness in his eyes that Roth understood at once. He softened his stance.

'Because we parted on bad terms.'

The chef said nothing, just stood in the doorway, holding Roth's gaze.

'This was years ago. A lifetime.'

'Then it's over,' the chef said. 'Leave her alone.'

146

'Yes,' said Roth, feeling the prickles in his chest. 'Of course.'

The chef shut the door as if it were a full stop. Roth thought carefully about his next move. He stepped out into the rain and heard it falling like tiny stars onto the brim of his hat. A kaleidoscope of neon colours reflected from the wet sidewalk, colours he had not noticed before. God had lifted the heavy cloak of darkness from his shoulders. The long night was over. God had brought Chiara back to him.

Anna kept the key she had found. She wondered if it might belong to the man in the fedora hat. That night she slept badly, and when she did sleep she woke each time thinking about him, this stranger who reminded her of a dead movie star. There was something about him that disturbed her. He was on her mind all the following day, making her so distracted even Luigi noticed. And now, that evening, he was standing inside the restaurant door, waiting for her to show him to a table.

She smiled shyly as she took his coat and hat. She knew he had come back, not for his key, but because of her. She could feel his eyes on her as she led him to the table she had kept free just for him. She could feel him watching her as she carried his coat and hat to the cloakroom. He could probably see her through the doorway, standing on tiptoe to reach the coat hook. She hoped he liked what he saw, despite her plain shift and flat shoes.

'Can I get you something to drink?' she said, returning with the menu. She felt self-conscious under his gaze. 'An aperitif while you're deciding what to order?'

She waited for him to say something. He was studying her like an oil painting, the impasto brushstrokes of her night-black hair, the delicate glaze of her pale skin. He looked dissatisfied, although she sensed his dissatisfaction had more to do with the skill of the artist rather than with the subject of the painting. She smiled.

'You remember me?' he said, his face unfolding in hope.

'Sure,' she said, thinking of the night before.

'But your accent,' he said. 'It's not right. You don't sound Italian any more.'

He creased his brow as he spoke, a squall of something more than puzzlement.

'My accent has never been Italian,' she said, sensing his disappointment like a stone in her own breast. 'You're mistaking me for someone else.'

He looked at her with a pain and an intensity that made her want to apologise for being who she was.

'The food is genuinely Italian, though. The chef is from Napoli.'

'You should be Italian,' he said.

She hesitated, wanting to ask him what he meant. His eyes grew shiny, sparkling with reflections of the candle on his table. With a start, Anna realised he was crying.

'I'll bring you a drink,' she said, and hurried away.

Through his tears, Roth watched her go. She looked exactly like Chiara, but she wasn't Chiara. She sounded nothing like her. The tone of her voice, her accent, everything was wrong. He dried his eyes on the napkin from the table. God had not brought his love back to him; He had played a terrible practical joke on him. Roth could imagine Him, laughing up His sleeve.

He remembered how he had first caught sight of her, a long sleepless night ago. He had stepped into the shelter of the doorway, felt the light against his face. She was a vision fragmented and distorted by the thick safety glass of the window in the restaurant doors. He felt as if he were under water, a sensation he had grown accustomed to over the

148

years. And, suddenly, there she was. She was all in black, Chiara's favourite colour. His heart flipped like a banked salmon. He gasped for breath.

'This is impossible,' he told himself, yet still he began to believe. The waitress had Chiara's eyes, as big and deep and blue as the Adriatic. Her hair, dark as her dress, was styled all wrong but otherwise it was the same. It seemed to him that she was a blessing from God Himself. It was as if He had given Chiara back to him. And it seemed that his love for her that he had kept buried so deep for so long had finally bubbled up to burst into the air around him. The sensation was so powerful, so strong, that it drained him, left him weak.

He watched her, now, walking away from him and going into the kitchen. He saw her hand, so small and so white, against the metal push-bar. He saw the pale curve of her neck beneath the dark bunch of her hair. She was just like Chiara and yet she wasn't Chiara. Nevertheless, that overpowering feeling was still throbbing in the air all around him. It was love, he thought, in its purest form. Love for this woman who was not, and yet who *was* his Chiara.

Anna stood at the bar, fingering the key, mulling things over. There were other diners to serve, but none of them needed her yet. It was another quiet night. She began preparing the man's drink. Luigi was watching her. He called her into the kitchen.

'What's going on with you and that guy?'

'Nothing,' she said. 'I was just getting him a spritz.'

'Who is he? He says he knows you. He told me last night you parted on bad terms, like the two of you were lovers.'

'I don't know who he is. But he has an aura of sadness about him.'

'What are you talking about?'

'Did you ever see that film, *Casablanca*? The one where Bogart does the noble thing and makes the love of his life leave with another man? He reminds me of Bogart, of how the character he played would have become, ten years after losing everything.'

She walked out before Luigi could say anything. When she returned to the man's table with the Aperol Spritz he seemed to have recovered, his head bowed over the menu.

'I think I have something of yours,' she said.

She placed the key on the table. He didn't look up. He was still quietly crying.

'Try this,' she said, placing the drink next to the key. 'On the house.'

He raised his eyes only as far as the glass of orange fizz. He seemed mesmerised by it. Then he lifted his face fully. His voice was tight, barely more than a whisper.

'Tell me that's not an Aperol with white wine.'

His look made her feel uncomfortable. She couldn't deny it. She wondered what she had done wrong. Slowly, he looked away from her, back to the menu. She waited.

'Do you believe in Destiny?' he said. He spoke downwards, almost into his lap, and she wasn't sure she heard him correctly.

'Destiny?'

It was the most ridiculous story Luigi had ever heard. And yet Anna, it seemed, had swallowed the whole thing. She seemed to believe this man really was Humphrey Bogart, or who Bogart's character would be ten years after *Casablanca*.

'But it's just a fantasy!' he said out loud.

'And this is the reality.' She spread her arms and turned a full circle in the small, shabby kitchen. 'If you're asking

150

me to choose between fantasy and reality then I choose fantasy, every time.'

'So that's it?' he said. 'You're leaving me, just like that?'

'He flies home to Italy in the morning,' Anna said. 'He told me he has a villa there. He asked me to go with him, and suddenly I could see that anything was possible. He had woken me up to the fact that there could be more to my life than this. I knew I had to seize the moment.'

She began collecting together the things she kept in the locker at the far end of the kitchen: hair brush, hand cream, spare tights, her purse.

'How do you think I'll manage without you?'

'You can easily get another waitress,' she said with her back to him. 'Like that.' She snapped her fingers.

'But what about *me*?'

At last, she turned to face him. Her mascara had run slightly, and that gave him a wisp of hope.

'You have your wife,' she said.

Luigi started to protest, to make idle promises, but he knew it was too late for that. He stopped talking.

'I'll miss you,' she said.

Luigi wondered if it was true, even if she meant it. He patted his chest, his trouser pockets, as if he were searching for the wallet he knew he didn't have on him.

'Let me settle up with you, at least. Let me pay you what I owe you.'

She straightened her back.

'You could never afford to pay me what you owe me, Luigi.'

Roth stood on the corner, waiting for her with his hands in his pockets, touching the cold metal firmness of the key she had given him. It started to rain again. He would be glad to leave this city. Tomorrow he would be home, in the warmth and the sun. His friends would notice at once the difference in him. They would say he was crazy when he told them the story of the waitress in the Italian restaurant and how she had unlocked his heart. They would tell him that he did not even know her. He didn't even know her name.

'Of course I know her,' he would say. 'She is my Chiara.'

Anna was in a taxi, heading through the rain to the airport. Tomorrow she would be miles away, somewhere warm and sunny. Somewhere where she could finally be herself. She wondered how long the stranger in the hat would stand on that corner, waiting for her, unaware she had left by the back door. She knew he would forget her in a day or two, or find another Chiara in another Italian restaurant. Even Luigi would learn to manage without her eventually.

Outside, the lights of the city slipped past, their neon colours captured in rivulets on the taxi window. She felt like Sleeping Beauty, awake after a hundred years, seeing the world through fresh eyes. She had no idea where she was going, or where she would end up. But she knew her destination was unimportant. The important thing was that she was, at last, going somewhere.

Bad Trip

Last night Steve was spaced, but this morning he feels kind of weird. Like, uncool, man. He has woken up in a strange place. Even though it's still dark he knows it's not his pad. It smells funny for a start. Not damp and fetid like his flat, but warm and fragrant. He feels kind of bloated, as if overnight all his muscles have filled with heavy water or something. His whole body is stiff, but when he touches his arms his flesh feels like stretched rubber, soft and flabby. He is wearing the kind of brushed cotton pyjamas he used to wear as a kid. The bed sheets are crisp and, well, clean. It could be a hospital, except now he can sense he's in a double bed, and he is now becoming aware of the sleeping woman beside him, becoming aware of her warmth and her sweetly scented skin . . .

What happened last night? His head is full of chemical residue, and he can't think straight. Joni called round straight from work, and they did some blow and then did the juicy. That was nice, lying in bed afterwards, stroking her beautiful hair. Then they went out and met some friends at the Chelsea Drugstore and had a few drinks. Someone gave him a couple of blues and they ended up on Old Brompton Road, downstairs at the Troubadour. Jimi Hendrix was there, making eyes at Joni until he got up and played Purple Haze for about fifty minutes. Then what? Steve thinks he might have dropped a tab or two of acid, but he isn't sure. Everything is getting hazy again.

He gets out of the bed and feels his way along a dark landing to the bathroom. When he pulls on the light he discovers that the pyjamas he is wearing cover a portly body that is most certainly not his. *What the fuck...?* The hands he holds up in front of him are porky too, something like his own hands but swollen and blotchy with liver spots. He realises he is gasping for breath, either from the exertion of his excursion to the bathroom or the shock of what he has found there. Or both.

He takes a tentative step towards the mirrored door of the medicine cabinet and finds himself looking into the heavily bagged face of an elderly man. 'What the fuck...?' he says out loud.

He opens the medicine cabinet. There are plasters and painkillers, Sterident and mouthwash, and a packet of something called Aricept, but no clues as to where he is or what has happened to him. He thinks the Aricept is important, but can't remember why. The arteries in this old man's head are popping and pounding, making him aware of an old heart pumping thin blood around this worn-out body. Making him aware of the proximity of mortality. How has this happened? He sits on the toilet seat and tries to make sense of it all. He had been reading Kafka yesterday, *Metamorphosis*. So he knows this is his mind playing a trick on him, a drug-driven, hallucinatory trick.

At least he isn't a cockroach.

He creeps down the carpeted stairs, into a dark hallway, finds the front door. Outside the sky is clear, but there are few stars. The suburban street is illuminated in patches by the streetlights. Strange looking cars line the road, and there's a rumble of traffic from all around. The pavement is cold under his feet, but he doesn't care. He heads off in a direction that he instinctively feels will lead back to his flat. He hopes Joni will still be there; she'll know what to do.

154

After turning two corners he finds himself on a main road, sleek cars making thudding noises, bright light from foreign-looking takeaways spilling into the street. A group of lads stand by a bus shelter, lit by the glow from a luminous poster. A policeman, wearing something like a black lifejacket, is talking to them, taking notes. The lads are dressed for the track although none of them seems to have been running. One of them spots him and calls something out but Steve doesn't understand the words. The policeman looks over at him, his lifejacket rising and falling in a visible sigh. Steve turns and starts to hurry away, but his new elderly legs are stiff and sluggish. The policeman catches up with him easily.

'Hello again, Mr Mogridge. Off on our wanderings again, are we?'

'What?' Steve finds it hard to catch his breath, 'How do you know me? What's going on?'

The policeman takes his arm, leads him towards a sleek patrol car. 'Don't you remember me? This is the third time I've had to deal with you lately. Aren't you a bit cold in those pyjamas?'

The interior of the car is warm and luxurious, really comfy seats. Steve has been in the back of a number of police cars in his time, drugs busts and such like, but never in anything as fancy as this one. 'Can't you just take me home?' he says as the policeman climbs into the driver's seat. 'I haven't done anything wrong. I'm just a bit . . . I don't know where I am or how I got here.'

The car makes the short drive back to the house he had left a few minutes earlier. The policeman's grip on his arm as they walk up the path is firm and inescapable. 'I don't want to go back in there,' Steve says. 'I want to go home. I want to go back to Shepherds Bush.'

The policeman ignores him politely and knocks on the

door. Lights come on, and Steve hears footsteps on the stairs. An old woman in a quilted dressing gown opens the door, her face as grey and dishevelled as her hair. She says, 'Oh God, not again,' and the policeman apologises as though it has all been his fault. Steve is taken to the back of the house, into a space-age kitchen with spotlights in the ceiling and sparkling appliances. The old woman fills a chromium kettle and apologises to the policeman, who laughs in a good-natured way.

'You need to put a child lock or something on the front door, Mrs Mogridge.'

Mrs Mogridge? What's going on?

'The consultant said this would happen eventually,' she says, 'but I didn't think it would be so soon. We're trying to find him a place in a residential care home. It's not what I want for him, but what can you do?' The kettle clicks, and turns itself off automatically. 'Tea or Nescafe?'

What has probably happened, Steve thinks, is this: that last tab of acid was so strong it must have released him from his body completely. Usually, when he was tripping and had an out of body experience and his spirit was up there on the astral plane there was still a link, a Golden Thread, back to his earthly body. Somehow, he had come unthreaded. Or maybe entangled. This old geezer was probably on the way out, about to peg out in his sleep, so his spirit had been released too in some kind of near-death experience, and the two of them had got their Golden Threads crossed. The result was he had come back down into the body of the wrong Mogridge. Fuck, does that mean this old bloke's soul is now in Steve's body, in bed with Joni? *Make the most of it, pal!* Jeez, what if he is really good at it? They say older men can keep it up longer. What if Joni prefers Steve's body with the old bloke inside? That settles it; he has to get

156

back into his real body as quickly as he can. And he realises now – it's so obvious! – that the way to get back is to take another trip, get back on the astral plane and untangle those Threads. First opportunity he gets he'll have to get out and score.

'Excuse me,' he says. 'But where are we?'

'You're at home, dear,' says the old woman.

'But I mean where's home?'

He clocks the old woman and the policeman exchange a knowing look. 'We're in Streatham, dear. This is our home. Remember?'

'Yeah, that's right. Streatham. And you're . . . not my mother. You're . . . what? My wife?'

Unaccountably, the old woman starts to cry. The policeman says, 'Yes, Mrs Mogridge is your wife. She looks after you.' He turns to the old woman. 'Would you like me to run him down to the hospital? See if I can get him admitted for the night?'

There's a brief discussion after which it is agreed that as long as Steve behaves himself there's no need for the policeman to take him anywhere. The old woman says she will be fine, and the policeman gives Steve a lecture on wasting police time when there are more important things to be dealt with.

'Like those lads by the bus stop?' says Steve. 'What were they up to? Dealing drugs, where they?'

'What makes you think that?'

Steve shrugs. 'I know I was a bit confused earlier but I'm okay now. I think I'll go back to bed.'

While the old woman is letting the policeman out, Steve pokes around in the wardrobe, getting a set of the old man's clothes together. He hides them in a drawer and climbs back into bed, feigning immediate sleep. He hears the old woman come into the room and hears her

157

turn out lights before getting into bed next to him. He feels her hand against his face. 'I do love you,' she says.

When her breathing has become rhythmic and sonorous, he carefully climbs out of the bed and silently retrieves the hidden clothes. Down in the futuristic kitchen he gets dressed as quickly as he can. The old woman's handbag is on the counter, and he guiltlessly removes her purse and slips it into his pocket. Outside, he retraces his steps back to the main road and the illuminated bus shelter. The lads have moved on, but it doesn't take him long to find them, openly smoking joints on a nearby street corner. They are white boys, but they talk like the West Indians up Notting Hill Gate.

'Are you guys selling?' he says. 'I'm interested in buying. I'm interested in doing some business.'

They laugh. 'We don't deal Viagra, man!'

He finds their guttural Jamaican cockney accents difficult to understand. 'I'm interested in some acid. Do you deal in that?'

'What's he saying? What are you talking, man?'

'Lysergic acid? LSD.'

They laugh again. 'Therapeutic acid, eh? You think it will make you better? Like them old ladies taking the weed for their arthritis.'

'Something like that.'

'We don't do that shit, man. No one does that shit any more.'

'So what do you do instead? I need to get high.'

They laugh and start mocking him, then one of them says, 'Sell him some crack, man.'

'Crack? What's that? I really need acid. It's very important.'

'Hey, chill out, man. You don't need acid when you got crack. But you is old, man. This stuff could kill you.'

'I'll take my chances. Give me ten bob's worth.'

'What you talking about?'

'He means fifty pee, man!'

'Fifty pee ain't enough. How much money you got in your lady purse? Let me see.'

'I – I don't know. It looks foreign.'

One of the lads takes a coin from the purse and hands it to him. 'This is fifty pee, man. Ten bob. You can keep that. But we'll take the rest in exchange for some rock and a free lesson in how to smoke it.'

'Are you ripping me off?'

'No way, man. You knows you can trust us.'

So he follows them into what looks like a disused squat, and smokes some rock.

When he comes to he finds himself back in bed. For a moment he dares not move, aware of the sleeping body beside him and afraid to look. His head is swimming. He opens his eyes and takes in the familiar ceiling. 'Thank God!' he says out loud.

'Steve?'

'Joni!'

'Oh, Steve! Thank heavens you've come back to me! I thought you'd gone for good.' She runs her hand over his face, kisses his cheek.

'That was a heavy trip, man. Really freaky!' He turns to face her, his Joni. He is overwhelmed by a surge of love for her. He begins to cry.

She kisses him tenderly on the forehead. 'Would you like some tea?'

He watches her pull on her quilted dressing gown and he tries to piece things together, to clear the fog from his brain and apply some logic to the bizarre sequence of events he has experienced over the past few hours.

Nothing has made sense but, hey, that's drugs for you. The sound of Joni making tea downstairs seeps into his consciousness, filling him again with that sense of oneness with her. It is then that he becomes aware of something digging into the palm of his hand, of his fist clenched tightly around it. Opening his hand he finds a silver-coloured coin, oddly shaped with seven sides. He looks up as the old woman comes back into their bedroom carrying two mugs of tea.

'Joni?' he gasps.

She tries to smile, but her face is lined with sadness, and her beautiful hair is grey and dishevelled.

Dos Cafes con Leche

Mr Morris came to the holiday island to escape from the emptiness of his life, but habit was a cruel and constant reminder of his loss. Today for example, sitting at a table outside a small restaurant in the heart of the resort, he had without thinking ordered *dos cafes con leche.*

'*Dos? Two* coffees, *senor?*'

He felt hot blood flood into the vessels in his cheeks, but he was damned if he would admit his mistake to this woman. '*Si, por favor,*' he said. '*Dos cafes.*'

The waitress shrugged, and went back inside. She probably thought he was a silly old fool. She was probably right. In due course she brought him two coffees. Mr Morris accepted one cup and indicated the vacant seat opposite his, nodding to the waitress as she placed the second coffee where his wife should have been sitting. He pretended to check his watch as though awaiting a delayed companion. The waitress stood appraising him, so he appraised her back. Fifty something, trim figure, not exactly a faded beauty but not unattractive, either, especially when she finally smiled at him.

'She is late, no?'

'She is indeed,' Mr Morris said.

He had to look away and the waitress, seeming to comprehend, retreated to another table of tourists. Mr Morris sighed and turned his attention to the hordes of people passing by, walking aimlessly back and forth along the harbour-front. He identified three distinct groups: the newly arrived couples, pasty-faced like him; the red-faced couples who must have arrived mid-week; and the brown-skinned couples just beginning their second week. He tried to spot the islanders among the strollers so he could watch where they chose to go to eat. Inside information was always useful. But all he could see were holidaymakers, like him. The only locals to be seen were serving in the many cafes and restaurants. Others would no doubt be cleaning floors and changing sheets in the hotels and holiday complexes that made up the rest of the resort.

'*Excusa, senora,*' he said as the waitress passed him on her way back from serving a table of German holidaymakers. He went on in Spanish, 'Is there a church near here?'

'Church?' the waitress replied in English. 'No, *senor.*'

Mr Morris cursed his inadequate Spanish grammar for the confusion. He had already noticed that none of the islanders he spoke to ever used Spanish when they replied to him, even if their English was worse than his Spanish. He wondered why that was. Reluctantly, Mr Morris addressed the waitress in English, which he felt to be at the least impolite and, at the worst downright offensive.

'Not here, of course. I can see there's no church *here*. But in this town. Where is the church in this town?'

'There is no church in this town, *senor*. The nearest church is in Buenaventura.'

'No church?'

'No, *senor.*' She nodded towards the untouched coffee, the empty chair. 'Your friend, she has deserted you?'

'Oh. Uh, yes. I suppose...' And then, because her smile seemed so warm, he said: 'Actually, there isn't anyone. Force of habit, you see? There's only me now.'

She nodded. 'Yes,' she said. I understand.'

And Rosa did understand, although she rarely allowed her feelings to rise to the surface. But there was something in

162

the demeanour of this tourist that she recognised in herself. A look in his eye, perhaps. She felt a strange connection with him, an inexplicable feeling that they had met before. Something in her belly fluttered like the first pangs of indigestion.

After a while, he called her over again.

'Another coffee, *senor*?'

'Er... yes, all right. But I wanted to ask you about the church. Is it really true there's no church around here?'

'Yes, it's really true. There is no need for a church.'

'But I don't understand.'

She laughed. 'No one lives in this town. It is just for the tourist. Everything just for the tourist. That is why there is no church.'

His befuddlement amused her, but without the contempt that usually accompanied her amusement at the ignorance of the English. She went to fetch another coffee.

'How far is it to Buenaventura?' he asked when she returned.

She was puzzled. 'Buenaventura? There is nothing at Buenaventura.'

'There's a church,' he said with a smile.

She could not understand why she found him less irksome than the rest of his compatriots. 'You are a religious man?'

'Not really. I just...' He shrugged. 'I just want to see the real island. *La vida auténtica*. Not this artificial tourist resort. Do you see?'

'Not really, *senor*. But if you are determined to see Buenaventura it's about twenty kilometres north.' She smiled again. 'Unless you go by taxi, when of course it will be more.'

'Of course,' he laughed, and she found herself laughing with him, with an English tourist.

Taken aback, she retreated quickly to the kitchen, where she could regain her normal air of detachment.

The trip to Buenaventura was immensely disappointing: breezeblock buildings, empty streets and a soulless church. Back in his *apartamento* he ran a defiant bath and soaked in the lukewarm water, thinking about the waitress he had spoken to in the restaurant that morning. She was the only pleasant islander he had met so far. She was quite attractive, too. A charming smile, beguiling eyes. Perhaps he would return to that restaurant for dinner.

He plunged his head under the bathwater, trying to force the thought from his mind. How could he think about another woman in that way? What would Vera think if she could see him now? What if she were able to read his lecherous thoughts? No! He was a widower, and he would behave accordingly. He would respect the memory of his wife, and drive the waitress from his mind. In any case, even though she was not much younger than he was, they were a world apart. She would not give him a second look, probably. He was old before his time, he knew. She was vivacious, with sparkling eyes and flashing teeth. And her figure...

He plunged his head beneath the water once more.

The restaurant was full tonight, mainly Germans and Dutch, good spenders. Rosa rushed to and fro, taking orders, serving meals, bantering with her customers and shouting at her staff, three of whom also happened to be her brothers and the owners of the business. But she was the boss; there was never any doubt of that.

A large group of German holidaymakers called her over and ordered several bottles of wine, and as she wrote their order on her pad her eye happened to glance across to the tables in Juan's section. A thin pale man, vaguely familiar, was sitting alone by the door, watching her. He smiled at her as he noticed her glance, but she looked away quickly.

'*Ja, vier flaschen rot wein.*'

She could feel his eyes on her as she moved through the tables. She felt self-conscious, and the fluttering in her belly grew stronger. As she looked in his direction again she saw him raise his hand, waving to her, smiling still.

'Juan,' she called. 'The customer by the door needs a menu!'

Mr Morris lowered his hand as the waitress turned away and went into the kitchen. One of the male waiters came over to him, bringing a menu.

'An aperitif, *senor*?'

He was disappointed not to be served by the waitress. He had foolishly felt he'd made a connection with her. Peevishly, he contemplated having a chilled sherry when the door swung open and a middle-aged couple dressed as teenagers walked in.

The waiter turned to the newcomers. 'I am sorry, *senor*, *senora*. We are full. No more room.'

'Aw, come on, dear,' the woman said to the waiter. 'I'm sure you could squeeze in two little ones.'

'I regret it is not possible, *senora*. Every table is taken tonight. Perhaps tomorrow?'

The woman took in the room, checking what the waiter had just told her. Then, to Mr Morris's horror, she caught his eye and approached his table.

'Thank God, a friendly face!' she said, loud enough for several people nearby to look up. 'You was on our plane this morning, wasn't you? Sunnytours? Staying up at the Las Dunas Oasis Holiday Club?'

Mr Morris said he was. The waiter, who had been brushed aside, attempted to say something but the woman pointedly ignored him.

'What a stroke of luck!' She pressed her palm against her fulsome breast. Her hair was bleached a brittle shade of orange and frizzed alarmingly from her head. 'I'm Belinda, and this is my old man, Barry.'

Mr Morris thought that the man looked too old to be called Barry, which he knew was a ridiculous thing to think. Barry certainly dressed much younger than Mr Morris would ever dream of dressing. Especially with his full-term paunch and, once he'd removed his baseball cap, his severely receded hairline.

'Pleased to meet you,' Mr Morris said, nervously extending his hand in their general direction. Belinda grabbed it and kept hold of it, making a peculiar gesture with her head and her eyes that he struggled to comprehend.

'Oh! I'm so sorry,' he said at last. 'My name's Morris.'

'Maurice! What a lovely English name! Well, I'm very pleased to meet you, too, Maurice.'

'No, I—'

'You don't mind if me and Barry join you, do you? Lovely!'

Belinda sat herself down at his table and motioned for Barry to join her. The waiter looked at Mr Morris with a helpless shrug and Mr Morris, equally helpless, shrugged back.

'Let's have three gin and tonics to kick off, and a jug of sangria to whet our appetites, eh?'

The waiter nodded and walked away, leaving Mr Morris to his fate.

Looking through the hatch from the kitchen, Rosa watched the Englishman at the table by the door squirm in the presence of his new companions. She recognised him now, and realised she must have appeared rude when she ignored him earlier. He was having a bad time, trying to enjoy the sangria his new friends had ordered but patently not doing so. She delivered paella to a table nearby and went across to say hello.

'Did you find your church, *senor*?'

He smiled bashfully. 'It wasn't quite what I had expected,' he said.

'Not very picturesque, no?'

'No, not very.'

She noticed the man and woman at his table exchange a knowing look, something he seemed to notice, too. He flushed slightly, nervously fiddling with his collar.

The woman said: 'Shall we have another jug of sangria?'

Rosa noticed his face drop at this suggestion. 'Your meal will be ready shortly,' she said. 'May I suggest a bottle of Rioja instead?'

'Why not make it two bottles,' the woman said. 'After all, we're on holiday, ain't we?'

'No problem.'

Mr Morris felt the room tilt, and grabbed a hold of the edge of the table. Belinda noticed what he'd done and laughed loudly, drawing attention to the three of them yet again.

'You're squiffy, Maurice. You've had one too many.'

'Leave him alone,' Barry said. 'He's on his holidays, ain't he?'

Being on holiday, it seemed to Mr Morris, was all the reason Belinda and Barry needed to behave loutishly. 'I'm not accustomed—'

'That waitress seems to have taken a shine to you, Maurice.' Belinda said. She tried to chuck him under the chin.

'Really? Do you think...?'

'I reckon you've pulled, my son.' Barry nudged him with his elbow.

'No, I don't...'

'See if you can get us a brandy or something on the house.'

The waiter appeared as if from nowhere. 'Would you like some coffee? Or the bill?'

'No, thank you, Pedro. We'd like some *booze*. Let's have some more sangria, shall we?'

Mr Morris could feel the eyes of everyone else in the restaurant boring into him and his table. Squiffy he may be, but Belinda and Barry were much farther gone. He did not want them to have any more to drink. He could see the friendly waitress looking at them all with disdain. She wouldn't be friendly for much longer.

'I think we should have the bill,' he said.

'No, no, no, Maurice. The night is jus' begging... beginning. It's still young. Like us, Bazza, eh? Young as the night.'

'Brandy,' said Barry, drawing a little circle in the air above the table, including Mr Morris in the round. 'Large ones.'

Mr Morris felt powerless, impotent. The waiter hesitated for a moment, then was gone. Mr Morris was trapped, with more alcohol coming. Belinda and Barry had spotted something in the waiter's demeanour that had amused them and they were now laughing almost beyond control, flesh-wobbling laughter that offended Mr Morris on so many levels that he felt he could no longer just sit idly by. He stood up.

'Do one for me while you're going, Maur.'

The waitress intercepted him as he approached the *servicio*. 'I shall send over the bill with your brandies, *senor*.' She looked annoyed.

'Yes, of course.' He wanted her not to be annoyed with him, but he knew he was guilty by association. 'Look, I'm sorry,' he said weakly.

She flattened her lips, giving him an inch. 'Your friends, they have had enough to drink.'

'Yes, too much. But I—'

'It would be better if you were to go, I think.'

He felt she must be disappointed in him, at his behaviour, but he had done nothing wrong. He was the innocent party in all this, as much a victim as anyone in the restaurant.

'Look, they aren't my friends, you know.' He placed a hand on her arm. 'I've only just met them.'

She moved her arm away, but not immediately.

'They are at your table, *senor*.'

'Yes, but I hardly know them.'

'But they are *with* you, *senor*. Your compatriots.' She was smiling at him now. Or was she just mocking him?

'They are simply sitting at my table. We are most definitely *not* together. They are nothing to do with me, and I am nothing to do with them.'

'No? But you come from the same country, speak the same language, share the same culture.'

Mr Morris was flabbergasted. 'Culture? I hardly think so!'

'It is undeniable. You are English; they are English. The same, no?'

'We are not the same at all. We are different in every way.'

'You are better?' She *was* mocking him.

169

'I am just different. I am more like you, I think. I feel I am more like you.'

'You do not know me, *senor*.'

'No, but I know I know enough to know I'd like to know you better.'

'Oh. 'No, you know, you know, you know'?' Her gently mocking laugh made him feel lightheaded. 'What do you know?'

'Well, I know you are beautiful,' he said.

It was the look on her face that made him realise what he had just said. He racked his inebriated brain scrambling for something sensible to say, to retrieve the situation, to rescue himself. But then she began to smile a new smile, a full smile that revealed her teeth and coloured her cheeks.

'You are very forward, *senor*.' But she was not complaining.

'Could I ... see you sometime?'

Again she laughed. He braced himself for her brush off. But she said, 'Yes. Why not? I would like that.'

There was a loud crash from the far side of the restaurant and Mr Morris was suddenly aware of the world around him again. Belinda had fallen to the floor, shrieking with laughter. Barry was trying, between convulsive giggles, to replace her toppled chair; a waiter was attempting to help Belinda stagger to her feet.

The waitress turned back to Mr Morris. 'Get your friends out of here, *senor*. Before they do more damage. I will bring your bill.'

Eventually the restaurant began to empty as people finished their meals and made their way off to nightclubs or to bed. Rosa had time now, time to contemplate this strange feeling she had within her, time to think about the Englishman with the obnoxious friends. She had offended him by suggesting that they were friends of his. English snobbery, she had to laugh! But he had been right, he *was* different from them. From a different time, almost. A more innocent time. She looked out through the restaurant windows. He was sitting on a bench, waiting for her. She felt like a girl again. She couldn't explain the attraction she felt towards him. He was funny looking, old fashioned. Worse, he was English! But she liked him, was drawn towards him. He *moved* her. She couldn't understand it. But she smiled as she cleared away another table and saw him sitting outside. He was waiting for her to finish for the evening, a small bouquet on his lap.

Mr Morris sat on one of the benches outside the restaurant, outwardly impassive but inwardly wrestling with the extent of his foolishness. Had he been foolish to tell her she was beautiful? He became embarrassed by the thought, but then remembered how she had smiled when he said it. And was he being more foolish for imagining that she might be interested in him, an old widower in an alien environment and out of his depth to boot? Would he compound that foolishness if he asked her for a date?

He remembered thirty years ago – no, longer – a tiff he and Vera had let get out of hand to the extent that she had walked off one night, saying she would never speak to him again. They had been together only a few weeks, but he had known then that she was the one for him. She had worked in a department store at the time, a large store in a provincial town. As coincidence would have it, it occurred to him now, Vera had been a waitress too. She had worked in the Silver Service Restaurant on the fifth floor of the department store. Black dress and white apron. She used to hate the uniform, but he always quite liked it. That was what the argument was about, he remembered now. Something stupid that got out of hand.

He had bought her flowers as a peace offering, waited outside the store until she finished work. He had seen it as a vigil of love. She had forgiven him the instant she had seen him standing there, wilted flowers in his cold hands.

And as a cold night-wind blew up the *Avenda del Generalisimo Franco* he felt nineteen again. Was that foolish?

She noticed her brothers were looking at her in a peculiar way as they prepared to leave. 'Is everything okay, Rosa?'

'Everything is fine.'

The brothers looked at each other, conspiratorially.

'What's going on?' she demanded.

'Those English, earlier. They were trouble.'

She smiled. 'They were English,' she said.

'You had an argument with one of them. The older man.'

'He wasn't so old, was he?'

'Did he offend you?'

She laughed. 'No. I offended him, I think. But it is no problem.'

'We worry about you, Rosa.'

'I know, Juan. But there is no need.'

'You are sure?'

She looked out the window.

'I am sure.'

They kissed her cheek and left her to lock up.

Rosa checked the windows and the back door. She checked everything in the kitchen was switched off, and that everything was where it should be. Then she collected what she needed and switched off the lights. She was excited, she realised. The fluttering inside her that had been there all evening was now almost audible. Could this all be the fault of one funny looking Englishman? She smiled to herself, shook her head as if to clear it. Could this really be happening to her, after all these years? Was her frozen heart melting at last? She laughed out loud at the absurdity of it all. She opened the door and stepped outside.

But he had gone. The street was deserted, suddenly quiet, and she shivered at a half-suppressed memory of another time and another place. Then she chided herself, cruelly. She had been a fool to think the Englishman had been waiting for her. More likely he was having a secret tryst with the obnoxious woman who fell off her chair. She walked across to the bench he had been sitting on. He had left the flowers behind. She picked them up and sniffed their scent. For a moment she contemplated keeping the posy, kidding herself that they *were* for her after all. But then she grew angry with herself, and pounded the flowers with her fists. Feeling a little better, she tossed the battered posy into the bushes behind the bench and set off for home.

Mr Morris watched the island fall away, his forehead pressed against the cool plexiglas of the aircraft window, and released a long sigh. As the plane climbed into cloud, he looked around the cabin at his fellow passengers; brown and red faced holidaymakers returning home after a week or two in the sun. He alone was still pale skinned - although that fact was hidden by the large triangle of white lint dressing taped across his nose. Such colour as he had was due mainly to the green and blue bruising around his eyes. People were whispering to each other about him, wondering aloud how he had come to look that way. A car accident, perhaps? A child sitting across the aisle was staring at him with the open fascination her parents could only reprimand and envy. The plane flew into a pocket of turbulence, dropping and recovering and dropping again, bouncing Mr Morris up and down in his seat so that he grabbed his bound ribs for fear that the wound might reopen itself. He felt the thick dressing beneath his shirt pocket.

The men had grabbed him from behind, one smothering his face and mouth, gagging any yells, the other two pulling him by the arms back over the bench. They forced him through the bushes and into a deserted car park.

'You English think you take everything you want, just come and take,' one of them said with his unshaven face pressed against Mr Morris' cheek. 'You think you bring money, we are grateful? This is how we are grateful.'

He hit him, very hard, in the stomach. Mr Morris doubled up, but the two men holding him tightened their grip, pulling him up straight again.

'You understand?'

Mr Morris tried to protest, to explain. A boot in the groin cut him short.

'We see you in the restaurant, with your arrogant friends, watching Rosa with lust in the eyes. We see you outside, waiting, waiting. To do what? To take? No, *senor*. Not tonight.'

Barely conscious, Mr Morris saw the knife flashing in the darkness. And then the pain was gone. He closed his eyes and tried to picture her face, but all he could see was a young girl. A young girl from another time, vaguely remembered until now.

Mr Morris opened his eyes. It was the same, familiar bad dream he had suffered for years; the same recurring nightmare about a terrifying struggle with Vera in a dark, deserted place. For years he had puzzled over how a tiff

174

over a black and white uniform had got so out of hand. All he ever wanted was to love her. But this time the waking served only to bring home the full weight of its horror. The dream had a different ending.

A change in the air pressure made the wound in his side ache. The plane was still climbing. In an hour or two they would reach London and its grey buildings, and its grey streets, and its grey ribbon of the river snaking towards the airport and the end of his holiday. A depression settled on him, but it was fleeting. He remembered the look on Rosa's face when he told her she was beautiful. He remembered her smile. It was the same smile, although tinged with concern, that he'd seen when he opened his eyes in the hospital. Her warm hand that gently squeezed his.

The plane skimmed over creamy clouds. Mr Morris closed his eyes and basked in the blue sunshine. He had gone to the island to escape from the sad reality of his life, but fate still had its surprises. Like the warm hand that gently squeezed his.

His thoughts were interrupted by the voice of the air steward offering a selection of hot and cold drinks. He did not want to turn away from the window, from the creamy clouds and the blue sunshine. He was half afraid he was only dreaming. But then he heard Rosa's voice and he knew it was true.

'*Dos cafes*,' she said to the steward. '*Con leche, por favor.*'

A Bit of Company

It was a Tuesday he called. I know it was a Tuesday because I'd just got back from the shops and I always go down the shops of a Tuesday because that's the day I draw my pension, and it saves a trip out later in the week. Anyway, the food's fresher earlier in the week. Also, I can pick up the TV Times and then I'm set up for the following week. Not that there's much on these days.

'Mrs Parsons?' he says.

'Who wants to know?' I says.

'Can I come in?' he says.

'Got any ID?' I says.

Well you can't be too careful these days, can you? Mrs Swift from the church was given a right going over recently by some feller who turned up on her doorstep asking to read the meter. Gas man, he said. I ain't got no gas, she said. That's all right, he said, we do electric too now. So she lets him in and he turns her over. Pension money, rent money, even her savings from the tin on her dresser. Silly old dear! How daft can you get, keeping your savings in a tin on the dresser? That's the first place they'll look.

Anyway, he shows me this ID card but I can't see what's on it, the print's tiny and I haven't got my glasses on. It's definitely his picture on it though, all official like.

'You'd better come in then,' I says. 'And wipe your feet!'

I don't let him come no farther than the scullery though. Well, you can't be too careful. Mind you, he looks on the level, if you know what I mean. Nice coat. And a proper shine to his shoes. You can tell a man's character by the shine on his shoes. In my day, if you couldn't see your face in a man's shoes you'd give him a wide berth. That's why there's so many young girls in trouble these days, if you ask me. No one bothers with shoes any more. They all wear these plimsolls.

'I need to ask you a few questions, Mrs Parsons.'

That shook me a bit, the way he suddenly came over all official. 'You sound like a policeman.'

'I'm a private investigator,' he says. 'Like it said on my ID.'

'I'll just put the kettle on,' I says.

'It's taken me a long time to track you down, Mrs Parsons. A lot of hard work went into finding you, I can tell you. A lot of slog. There wasn't much to go on.'

'Could you get me the good teapot down from the dresser dear?' I says. 'As I've got company I might as well.'

He had to stretch a bit to reach the teapot. And then he tried to wipe the dust off it before handing it over, but of course it wasn't a dry dust, it was a greasy dust. It just stuck to his fingers. So he stood there with this black muck on his fingers, not wanting to wipe them on his fancy coat and I don't suppose he had a hanky.

'You'd best wash your hands in the sink,' I says, 'while I give this a wipe.'

His face was a picture.

'Nice view from this window,' he says, which was a bit of a fib because it just looks out over the communal garden and no one's done anything with it for donkey's years. It's all weeds and brambles. 'How long have you been living here now?'

'Can't remember,' I says. 'About twenty years, I suppose.'

'I think you'll find it was 1991 you took on the lease.'

'Really?' I says. 'It seems longer.' I spooned tea into the pot, after I'd warmed it of course, and poured in the hot water. 'Why are you asking if you already know the answer?'

'I need to check the facts, Mrs Parsons. You have to help me with the facts, corroborate the evidence.'

'I see,' I says, getting the cosy out the drawer.

'For instance,' he says, 'I need to check the date you became Mrs Parsons.'

I was setting out the cups and saucers on the table, sugar in a bowl, milk in a jug. I had been thinking about laying out some custard creams on a little plate, had even gone to get the biscuit tin from the cupboard.

'What are you on about?'

'Well,' he says, 'when did you get married to *Mr* Parsons?'

'Oh,' I says. 'It must be nigh on sixty year ago now.'

I opened the tin anyway and took out half a dozen biscuits. I do like a custard cream. They're a little bit of luxury. They're not too hard, like a gingernut say. My teeth can't cope with a gingernut. Not unless I dip it in my tea first, give it a bit of a soak. Then it just melts in your mouth. But you can't dip biscuits in your tea when you've got company, can you? It's not polite. But a custard cream is that bit softer. And I like the filling. It's not really custard of course, it's not Bird's. I suppose it's a kind of fondant really. I don't know why they call it custard, making out it's something it isn't. But I like it anyway.

'Just after the war, then?' he says.

'About then,' I says.

'Only I couldn't find a marriage certificate.'

'What would you be wanting with my marriage certificate?'

'Evidence, Mrs Parsons. I deal in hard facts; my clients expect nothing less. Hard facts and corroborated evidence.'

179

Some people say you should pour the tea into the cup first, and then add the milk. That's the proper way. Some people get on their high horse about doing things the 'proper' way. Snooty people, like Mrs Swift, look down their noses at you if you put the milk in the cup first. I don't see as it matters much really but they think they know better.

'Lovely tea,' he says.

'Shall we take it through to the front room?' I says. 'It's more comfy in the front room.'

I hadn't put the fire on so it was a bit chilly. I generally turn it on around tea time, just after Countdown, so it's nice and warm by the time Emmerdale comes on. I can't afford to have it burning every hour of the day. But as I had company I lit it early.

'That's a pretty bird,' he says. 'Is it a canary?'

'It's a budgie,' I says. 'Canaries are yellow. Different bird entirely.'

'Are you a bird fancier then, Mrs P?'

'Not really. They're just good company'

He didn't say anything to that, just sipped his tea.

'Ah, this must be your son,' he says, standing up and taking the framed photo of my Colin from the mantelpiece, the one he sent with his last letter. It was a group photo, him and his wife, except I cut her half off. It's just Colin in the frame.

'This must be an old picture,' he says.

'Yes,' I says. 'Taken in Australia, just after he emigrated.'

'1968?'

'About then.'

'Got anything more recent? Pictures of the grand-children?'

'No,' I says, 'nothing like that.'

He took a custard cream from the plate and sat down again, dipping it in his tea. He was thinking about something so I didn't interrupt him. It was nice to have the company.

'Look, Mrs Parsons,' he says. 'I'll stop beating about the bush. I've been trying to track you down for nearly a year now. I've got some news for you. Something that will be very much to your advantage.'

'You've gone all official again,' I says.

'How would you like to fly out to Australia, visit your son?'

'That would be a fine thing, I'm sure. How would I do that at my age? I doubt I'd get as far as the airport!'

It's bad enough getting down to the shops and back. It's a terrible struggle; I get so short of breath. I don't like to trouble the doctor. Mrs Swift reckons it's angina but I told her it's my chest. Plus I've got that Austrian arthritis.

'Well maybe your son and his family could come over to England to visit you,' he says. 'Maybe you could treat them.'

'I do like a comedian,' I says. 'You should be on the stage.'

'Mrs Parsons, do you remember a man called Marvin Campbell?'

Well, I did come over queer!

'Scotch, is he?' I says.

'American,' he says. 'I think you met him during the war. He was stationed over here, not far from where you were brought up in Hampshire.'

'Would you like more tea?'

'That would be lovely, thanks.'

It was a struggle to stand up, I can tell you. It was like all the energy had been drained from me. The cups were rattling in their saucers as I carried them back to the scullery. I poured out the tea and then found my bottle of medicinal brandy in the cupboard, added a large dash to my cup, stirred it in. Perhaps I should have put the brandy in first.

Back in the front room I says: 'I've been racking my brains. I don't remember anyone called Campbell. I think you've made a mistake. I've always lived in London. I went to Hampshire on my holidays once, I think. Didn't meet no Yanks.'

'Before you, er, got married you were known as Pirbright, I think. According to the records you didn't move to London until after the war. After your son was born, in fact. That seems to be when you became Mrs Parsons.'

'I don't know what you're talking about, I really don't.'

He put his tea down and leaned forward, all earnest like. 'Marvin Campbell returned to America in 1946. He got married and settled in Iowa, where he started a small electrical business. Over the years the business grew, and expanded into computers, and Marvin Campbell became a very wealthy man. A multi-millionaire, in fact.'

'That's nice,' I says. What else could I say?

'Mr Campbell passed away last year.'

'Oh.'

'He left a small fortune.'

'I see.'

'And part of that small fortune, a not insignificant part, he left to Alice Pirbright, the mother of his illegitimate son in England.'

I drank all the rest of my tea in one go. The brandy warmed the tubes all the way down to my tummy, and at the same time seemed to fill my head with air.

'Marvin Campbell's attorneys employed me to track down Alice Pirbright. And now I have. Congratulations. You're rich.'

I would have liked more tea, more brandy. But I knew I wouldn't be able to get to my feet for a while. So I just sat for a moment or two.

At last I says: 'I've always lived in London. My husband died in the war. I've never met no one called Marvin Campbell.'

His face!

'I know it's you, Mrs P. I've got the documentary evidence.'

I looked down at the tealeaves in my empty cup, trying to read what they said. 'What if you don't ever find this Alice Pirbright?'

'The will stipulates that if you hadn't been traced within a year of his death then his widow would have got everything.'

'And what about you? Do you still get paid for looking for her, even if you don't find her?'

'Yes,' he says. 'I still get my fee. But I *have* found you, so that's irrelevant.'

'It's not me,' I says. 'I'm a decent woman. My son's a decent legitimate man. I never had no children out of wedlock. I never went with no Yank, shiny shoes or no shiny shoes. I've always lived in London.'

'But we're talking about hundreds of thousands of pounds!'

'What good would all that money be to me?'

He held up the photo. 'You could see your son, for a start. Your grandchildren. You could buy a nice new flat, maybe one of these new retirement homes with wardens to do all your shopping or whatever. You wouldn't have to worry about money ever again. I know you're Alice

183

Pirbright, I can prove it. All I need is your signature on a piece of paper and all your troubles are over.'

The trouble with people today, it seems to me, is that they think money's the answer to everything. Mrs Swift says it's the root of all evil, and I reckon she's right. I managed to get to my feet at last.

'You got the wrong old bird,' I says. 'Sorry I can't help you.'

It was like it was his turn to get stuck in his chair. Eventually he stood up, but he didn't seem to want to go.

'No one need ever know,' he says. 'About your past, I mean.'

'I'm sorry you've had a wasted journey,' I says.

He gave me his card before he left. 'In case you change your mind,' he says. 'But you'll have to be quick. You're running out of time.'

When he'd gone I had another little drink of brandy, and sat at the scullery table to catch my breath. He seemed a nice man.

And then I remembered Mrs Swift, and what had happened to her, and I had a bit of a turn. I felt such a fool. I'd left him alone in the front room all that time, he could have got up to anything. But when I checked the back of the birdcage it was all right. My funeral money was still there, safe and sound. Everything was just as it should be.

Time to Kill

Just before the house lights came up, Jim suppressed a yawn. Up on the stage, a woman wearing a cardigan and black wellington boots was describing her mother's dying moments. Jim surreptitiously checked his watch. It hardly seemed to be moving. Chrissie touched his arm and, leaning close to his ear, said, 'Are you enjoying it?'

'Great,' he whispered back.

Was this what it meant to go straight? Killing time through interminable poetry readings by Chrissie's students followed by polite conversation with her colleagues from the university? This, apparently, was what it meant to be part of normal society, now he had decided to settle down with her. This, and the endless, fruitless job interviews. He had too much time on his hands. Sometimes, he wondered what Chrissie saw in him. Sometimes, he wondered what he saw in her. It had been different when he was inside and she was the visiting creative writing tutor. Then it had been all about bottle-up sexual desire. Now the cork was out the bottle and everything had gone flat.

Chrissie's Head of Faculty, a dry old bird with a severe haircut and a head that twitched and bobbed, applauded enthusiastically and Jim realised the poet was leaving the stage. He clapped his hands together. Her head darted in his direction and he made his mouth into a smile and looked away again. Another woman was getting to her feet off to the left, gathering sheets of paper together, preparing for her turn to hold forth about things Jim would never understand.

The event was taking place in a former medieval church, now converted into a secular arts centre and part-time nightclub. Their table was at the front, almost abutting the lip of the apron. He felt suddenly exposed as the darkness faded, as if all the people applauding behind him had turned their attention on him. As if they were analysing *him* for hidden meaning.

Chrissie's boss from the university was talking to him now. Talking down to him. She was explaining the difference between metaphor and simile. He would like to throttle her. He could happily wring out her turkey wattle like a wet towel.

'I'm going to the bar,' he said, not bothering to hide his irritation. 'Can I get either of you anything? More wine?'

Chrissie and her friend both shook their heads. There was a nearly-full bottle of screw-top Pinot Grigio on the table. They both still had wine in their glasses.

'Go easy,' Chrissie said to him. 'Don't forget you've got that interview in the morning.'

Jim got to his feet, beer glass in hand. Chrissie's friend whispered something in her ear. She was looking up at him as she spoke.

There was no real crush at the bar, but the service was slow. A woman was standing in front of Jim, asking for a glass of red wine and a mineral water. She noticed him and gave him the sort of smile that made Jim wish he had been on his own. He tried to smile back, but he was still irritated with Chrissie. Why had she made him come to this thing, anyway? And why had she insisted on bringing her boss along? His irritation tightened his smile into a grimace.

'This thing is much more popular than I expected,' the woman said to him as he ordered a pint over her shoulder. 'I wouldn't have guessed poetry would be such a draw.'

'Yes, there's a lot in tonight,' he said. Polite enough, but not bothering to try too hard.

'And not one of them smokers!'

She had turned to face him fully now, and he saw she was about his own age, early forties. She was a good-looking woman. Her eyebrows, he noticed in particular, had been plucked and trimmed into perfect arches. Her lipstick was probably a shade too red, but it went with her too-black hair.

'Do *you* smoke?' she said.

'Not anymore. I used to be a smoker. I gave it up.'

The woman seemed to find that amusing. She turned away from the bar, a glass in each hand. She took a couple of steps and stopped, waiting for him to collect his own drink. She was about six inches shorter than Jim, slightly built under a heavy winter coat. The rim of her wine glass now carried a smear of her lipstick, a little red moon.

'No one smokes anymore,' she said as he joined her. It was almost an accusation.

For some reason, Jim felt a sour tug of guilt. He should make his way back to his seat next to Chrissie. The bar area was in the east transept of the old church. Any remaining religious effigies were hidden behind posters of comedians or up and coming rock bands. Beyond a partition, spotlights hung from sacred beams. The stage was where the west transept must once have been. He could see Chrissie and her friend in animated discussion at their table in the front.

He should get back to his seat next to Chrissie. But for some reason he didn't want to be rude to this woman. He would exchange a few polite words with her, then excuse himself. She was probably thinking the same thing. She probably wanted to take the glass of water back to whoever it was she was with.

'Are you a poet?' she said.

Jim shook his head. In different circumstances he might have said something about Chrissie being the poet, but now for some reason he couldn't bring himself to mention her.

The woman said, 'I would have thought the only people interested in poetry these days, or at least interested enough to come to an event like this, would be poets themselves.' She lifted the other glass to her lips, the one containing the iced water, and Jim realised she was on her own. Both the drinks were hers.

'Are you, then?' he said, feeling a sudden, inexplicable excitement. 'A poet, I mean. Are you a poet?'

'Not any more,' she said. 'Like you and smoking, I gave it up.' She smiled at him, the way she had smiled earlier. 'Unlike you and smoking, though, I've decided to start again.'

The way she said it, the way she looked at him when she said it, made him feel that giving up smoking had revealed a flaw in his character, a lack of stamina or self-resolve. He was a quitter. He gave up too easily. What other things had he given up since he'd regained his freedom?

'Will you do me a favour?' she said.

It irritated him when people asked closed questions like that. It always made him want to say no. He shrugged instead, meaning whatever she wanted it to mean.

She held up the glasses, the water and the wine, demonstrating both her hands were full. 'Will you open the doors for me? I need to go outside for a smoke.'

He followed her and held the doors open, then without thinking about it he went outside with her. It was dark but it wasn't cold. There were no stars. When she sat down on the low wall around the church Jim sat down beside her.

'Why did you give up?' he said as he watched her forage in her handbag for her cigarettes. 'Poetry, I mean.'

'I got married,' she said.

He nodded, as if that explained everything.

'Worse thing I ever did.'

She found the pack and tapped the bottom, offering one to him. He shook his head, but watched her carefully as she took a cigarette and placed it between her lipsticked lips, clicked her lighter alight and sucked the flame against the tobacco. Her face was briefly lit up in the dark, and the soft glow was kind to her, much kinder than the harsh light in the bar had been. Then she clicked back into darkness, exhaling with a loud satisfied sigh. He found himself trying to breathe in the wisps of blue smoke that trailed from the corner of her mouth. She put the lighter down on top of the cigarette pack next to her on the wall. He noticed the way her dark hair curled forward beneath her ears. He noticed her earrings. He pictured her taking them off, placing them carefully on her bedside table.

'I married a bloody actuary! Can you believe that?'

She took another drag, the orange tip flaring aglow.

'An actuary!' she said, then let out a long stream of exhaled smoke. 'I haven't written a poem for twenty years. But now I think it's time I picked up on my life again. Doing things for myself at last.'

He looked away from her face, following the movement of the cigarette as she rested her hands on her lap. Her unbuttoned coat had fallen either side of her legs. Her skirt, he noticed, had ridden halfway up her thighs. He allowed himself to examine her enmeshed knees. He found himself wondering whether she was wearing tights or, perhaps, stockings.

'So,' she said. 'What do you call yourself these days?'

Jim felt something inside his ribs tumbling over. 'What's that supposed to mean?'

'You know exactly what it's supposed to mean. You think this was a chance meeting?'

'My name is Jim. Jim Thompson.'

'Really? Does that mean you've changed your line of business, as well as your name?'

He looked away from her. Decided not to argue with her. But he didn't get up. He stayed sitting on the wall.

'I'm not a poet,' she said. 'I need a job doing and you came highly recommended. My husband is very rich, and I enjoy having his money, but I can't stand being tied to him anymore. And yet if I divorce him I'll have nothing. So I can't afford to leave him. Do you understand? He is very well insured. In his line of business . . .'

'You've got the wrong man,' Jim said.

She didn't speak, but took a long drag on her cigarette, staring straight ahead.

'This building,' she said at last. 'What is it?'

'It's an arts centre. They have music sometimes. Jazz.'

'That right? Still looks like a church to me.'

'It used to be a church, but now it's an arts centre.'

When she turned to him her eyes were like ice. 'It might call itself something else, but it's still what it is.'

She held him in her frozen gaze for a moment.

'So why did *you* give up?' she said. 'Smoking, I mean.'

He looked away from her altogether, averting his eyes and thinking back, thinking of Chrissie complaining about him tasting like an old ashtray.

'The same reason everyone gives up,' he said.

'Do you believe all that stuff about cancer and heart disease?'

He checked her face to be sure she was being serious. She took the last drag from her cigarette and dogged it on the wall.

'Yes, I suppose I do,' he said.

190

'So why is it then that some people who smoke live to be ninety and some people who don't still die before their time?'

'I don't know,' he said.

'My husband never smoked. He has calculated he'll probably live into his nineties, maybe longer. Hardly reassuring. But not only cigarettes kill. There could be other factors he hasn't taken into account.'

He wanted to go back inside now, back into the warm. She didn't get it. He wasn't in that line of business anymore. He had changed. He hadn't given up smoking because he was afraid of getting cancer. He had given up because Chrissie hadn't liked the smell of it on his breath, in his clothes. You don't give up anything for yourself, he thought. The only reason you ever give up anything is simply because you want to make someone else happy.

'There's a doctor in America,' she went on. 'Some kind of anti-exercise nut. He reckons every human heart is pre-programmed to beat a certain number of times. And when your heart reaches that pre-ordained number of beats, that's it. It stops. And you die.'

'Just like that?'

'Just like that. He says you shouldn't take any form of exercise, or do anything too exciting, or engage in any kind of risk. Anything that raises your pulse rate would simply be wasting your allotted number of heart beats.'

'Is that right?'

'So he reckons.' She shifted her weight towards him and laid a hand on his arm. 'So just sitting out here with you, honey, with you making me feel the way you're making me feel, could be seriously damaging my health. It's just as well we're only talking!'

He wasn't sure how to take that, but he laughed politely.

She leaned closer still, and for a moment he could imagine letting himself go and kissing her. But he turned his face away just in time.

'Don't you think,' she whispered, her lips brushing against his ear, 'that it's the taking of risks that makes us human? It proves we're *alive*.'

He found himself looking at her knees again. She squeezed his arm, holding on to him a second longer than he expected, then released him and reached for her cigarette pack.

Later that night, when he and Chrissie arrived home, Jim was unusually aroused and wanted to go straight to bed. Chrissie, though, put the kettle on for tea, eager to talk about some of the poets they'd heard, her ex-students. She said poetry went to the heart of what it meant to be human. He stood behind her, stroking her hair, his eyes closed, and kissed the nape of her neck. The kettle switched itself off but she didn't make any tea.

In bed, naked, he enveloped her completely and kissed her with the old passion.

'Ugh!' she said, drawing back. 'Have you been smoking?'

'Of course not,' he said.

Chrissie rolled away from him, onto her side of the bed. Jim thought of the woman with the cigarettes, the woman whose phone number was on the torn-off strip of cigarette packet in his jacket pocket. He imagined he was in bed with her, and it filled him with an odd nostalgia. He lay thinking of all the things he had given up for Chrissie, listing all the things he had traded off to be here now, in this bed, in this flat, with this woman.

He turned towards her but Chrissie slipped out from under the duvet and left the room. He heard her go into the bathroom. He heard her lock the door, and then run a bath.

As though she wanted to wash away all trace of him. Was she ticking items off a list too?

Jim began to feel empty and sick, a sour taste in his chest. A silence descended on the bedroom. In the dark stillness, he believed he could hear his life passing him by. Perhaps it was the faint pulse of the second hand on his electric alarm clock, ticking off the passing moments. Or perhaps it was his own heartbeat, counting down, counting down. He'd been wrong earlier, thinking he had too much time on his hands. He had less and less.

He thought again of the woman he'd met tonight. He thought about her earrings and imagined her taking them off. He pictured her sitting on the side of her bed and rolling down her stockings. Then he thought about the phone number in his pocket and the woman's dull, rich husband, the excitement of being back in the game. He thought about it all for a long, long while.

And, as he lay there in the dark, he knew that in the morning everything would change.

www.ingramcontent.com/pod-product-compliance
Lightning Source LLC
Chambersburg PA
CBHW021038130626
46552CB00005B/1905